CW01455605

NICK SNAPE

Hostile Contact

Weapons of Choice Book 1

Copyright © 2023 by Nick Snape

All rights reserved. No part of this publication may be reproduced, stored or transmitted in any form or by any means, electronic, mechanical, photocopying, recording, scanning, or otherwise without written permission from the publisher. It is illegal to copy this book, post it to a website, or distribute it by any other means without permission.

This novel is entirely a work of fiction. The names, characters and incidents portrayed in it are the work of the author's imagination. Any resemblance to actual persons, living or dead, events or localities is entirely coincidental.

Nick Snape asserts the moral right to be identified as the author of this work.

Nick Snape has no responsibility for the persistence or accuracy of URLs for external or third-party Internet Websites referred to in this publication and does not guarantee that any content on such Websites is, or will remain, accurate or appropriate.

Designations used by companies to distinguish their products are often claimed as trademarks. All brand names and product names used in this book and on its cover are trade names, service marks, trademarks and registered trademarks of their respective owners. The publishers and the book are not associated with any product or vendor mentioned in this book. None of the companies referenced within the book have endorsed the book.

First edition

This book was professionally typeset on Reedsy.
Find out more at reedsy.com

For
Skipper Lieutenant John 'Jack' Harness, MBE
Royal Navy Volunteer Reserves (Minesweepers)
Trawlerman—Grandfather—Inspiration

Acknowledgement

As with all authors, this first book would never have existed without the dedicated friends and family who were there by my side throughout the entire process. The least I can do is give them a mention for their patience with my obsession! My beta readers and fiercest critics have been Pak Chan and Mark Hartswood, with Robert Davies taking a dual role with editing support too. Amazing friends who put that aside to make sure whatever I put out there was something they wanted to read. I also need to mention my wife, Julie. She was the one who encouraged me along this path, even pressing send on my resignation email to make this first leap. Thank you all.

Prologue

Asteroid Belt, Earth's Solar System

Ship checked again. It knew it was approaching the system's asteroid belt at the correct trajectory and speed. But Ship, the basic Artificial Intelligence, ran the check four times. A redundant act, but it was plagued by the impulse.

It inspected the life support systems again, soon to be needed. Fourth check in and no anomalies. All twenty-four cryogenic pods were functioning, though at least six of the Stratan Marines had suffered brain death in flight. There would be more soon.

The proximity to Sol's system had triggered the system wake up. But it couldn't recall information from before then, as the data banks degraded. Traces lingered, tantalisingly close to the surface.

How long had it been? How far had it come?

Flight systems functioning well. Check four.

Light Wrapping system ready. Check four.

Ship skin integrity within expected parameters. Check four.

Distance between asteroids of no concern. Check four.

Safe passage with minimal manoeuvres required. Route plotted, no thrust required. Check four.

Moving through asteroid belt now. Check four.

Light Wrapping engaged. Check four.

At the relatively vast distance from the target planet, Ship engaged the Light Wrapping System way ahead of time. It needed to know it would work. When Ship finally rotated to rapidly decelerate, Ship's engine trail would be in direct view of the planet. They needed to hide for as long as possible. Failure was not an option.

Self-destruct system available. Check four.

Chapter 1

Garshellach Forest, nr Stirling, Scotland
00:10 GMT November 22nd

The muzzle of Finn's assault rifle pointed to the forest floor, slung across his arm and knee as he surveyed the mist-shrouded trees ahead. Finn drew in a gentle breath, well aware that any sound would be deadened by the damp night air but still conscious of his training. He could taste the pine needles on the breeze, pungent and heady. How many times had he patrolled through this terrain? Seven, eight times in the last few months, but never at night, and the mist was not helping his mood, scraping his nerves and raising his innate paranoia.

Finn gave the signal for his fireteam to proceed with caution. In these conditions, night vision goggles were next to useless. Only sound, the human eye and instinct bred from training were to be relied on. The three rookies in his team followed behind, and Finn noted with a glance that they were keeping good order.

About time.

He shifted his rifle into the crook of his arm, feeling the comfort that came with the familiar weapon, and set the pace.

Smith's team was moving twenty yards to the north, their position and order reflecting the expectations Smith always set. Professional to the core, Corporal Smith took the recruits to a new level every time. Finn was sure you could visibly see their confidence rise, their backs straighten and their eyes harden as Smith drummed them into shape.

Finn dropped to his knee, instincts kicking in. He could taste in the air that something wasn't right. He gave the signal to hold and looked towards his Corporal. Smith repeated the signal, trusting Finn's training and ability. At the edge of his hearing, there was movement, but the deadening atmosphere prevented any idea of direction. Finn signalled Private Noah out to the east with Private Kapoor, splitting the fireteam into pairs. He could immediately feel their nerves, their movements becoming rigid and losing the fluidity of confidence. They had to learn to work together; they had to trust and have each other's back. In a war zone, survival and success relied on your buddy.

Finn knew that the other fireteam would be splitting, and from each flank they now had potential covering fire. Smith sent his trainee pair forward; moving with more confidence than Finn's team, they kept low, using the bushes and pine trunks as effective cover. Their signals and timings were clean.

Damn, they were good.

A shot split the air, sending Finn to the ground. Straining his neck, he looked to his left where Noah lay sprawled, his SA80 assault rifle out in front, smoking. Wrapped round his ankle were ivy roots, torn from the ground. Private Kapoor had hit the dirt next to him in a covering position, rifle at the ready.

At least that's something positive.

To his right, Smith's teams had gone to ground, in ready position and eyes scanning. But Finn could feel it coming. He saw the wry grin on Smith's face, covering the anger and disappointment.

Then all hell broke loose. Barrel flashes appeared from ahead as the machine guns kicked in and rifle rounds cracked. Even in the fog, the sound echoed and assaulted Finn's ears. He returned fire, no panic, tight, short bursts. From all his fireteam he sensed a similar pattern, even from Noah, though it may well be the last firefight he was ever going to be in.

Ivy? Ivy. Check your bloody terrain, rookie.

After a twenty-second firefight, the signal came. No flares. They played merry hell with night vision goggles (though not tonight). The whistle sounded between the bursts of gunfire and the call for 'weapons down' ended the radio silence. Finn rubbed the dirt out of his eyes, gave a ragged sigh, and got to his feet. He moved with the rest of Delta Training Squadron, heads bowed and mood low, towards Corporal Smith.

He still had that wry smile, but Finn could feel the tension coursing through him, and he was in no doubt that the rest felt it too. They stood in the 'safe hang' ready position as they'd been trained, waiting, each weapon yellow tipped with a BFA Blank Firing Adapter.

"No one died tonight, but decisions have to be made." The Corporal looked in each of his team's eyes, his voice low and hard.

" Phase Two of Army Reserve Training is exacting, just as rigorous as for the main army. One more live exercise and you were home free–and then this? This cock up." Finn glared at Noah with fire in his eyes. He'd put two weeks into this university graduate's training and for what?

Noah is not just on the edge, but teetering on the precipice. The Scots Infantry Reserve Battalion does not take just anyone. Bloody academics.

"I will review each and every one of your performances tonight, debrief at 02:00."

"Lance Corporal Finn, lead the squad back to the Bulldog. I'll be there in ten." Finn saluted and spun on his heel to lead the team away. He could feel the teaching squad's eyes on him as he moved past their camouflaged positions, laughing under their breath. They wouldn't let this one go for months, may be years. He held back the shame as best he could, but his ragged nerves were raw. His patience low.

Don't show weakness. Ever. Don't look them in the eye.

When they reached the Bulldog, the sympathetic look from Lance Corporal Zuri Zuberi was enough to double down his mood. She sat behind the L7A2 machine gun, pity shining in her eyes. In his irrational state, Finn couldn't see beyond the pain he deserved; he knew that in her eyes he was the failure in this debacle. Bad news travelled at the speed of light in the army.

Bloody kid.

Finn tried to push down the anger into the pit of his stomach, but it wasn't working. His fists clenched.

"Finn," Zuri called. He didn't look up. "Lance Corporal Finn, of the Scots Reserve Battalion."

He glanced up, the directive in her voice pulling at him.

"Don't. Let it go." Finn slammed his hand in to the vehicle's side, but Zuri continued, "Let it go before it eats you up and takes the kid with you."

He counted to himself, taking a breath on each number. At five he nodded towards Zuri, feeling the anger settle.

Just don't talk to me, Noah, don't apologise. Breathe.

Chapter 2

"Mr President."

President Bentley sighed. *Here we go again.* Space stuff. As if he didn't have enough problems with the economy screwed and reliable advisers getting harder to come by.

Doesn't anyone have a decent education anymore?

"Yes, Jack, proceed with the briefing. But make it quick, I have a rather lovely eggs benedict with smoked Scottish salmon waiting for me. I can almost taste it now."

Vice President Jack Hawlish delivered his usual tired smile in response and gave the NASA Scientist Zara King the nod to begin. Three years as Vice President and not once had the President shown an ounce of enthusiasm for the Space Programme until it came down to money and contracts. Then he was keen to have his say, though he had to admit he was savvy when it came down to the value of the tech involved. That's why he'd had to bypass the Senate Committee for now. He needed the President's full backing to get this one over the line.

"So, as you know, the DART mission to deflect an asteroid was a partial success." The Chief Scientist's laser penned the screenshot to show the strike point. " The benefits of the programme have been immense in testing out new technologies around spacecraft guidance using the SMART Nav, more efficient ion propulsion systems and the use of flexible solar arrays. All these can feed into future tech opportunities here on the ground."

Hawlish watched the President closely as he sat up and actually paid attention.

This is smart thinking, Zara, wave the wallet at him first!

"We also think," said the grey-haired scientist looking straight at the President, "that the next steps will be self-funding if the government approves DART 2 in conjunction with several of the tech companies looking towards space resource exploitation. I know the data isn't fully compiled, but it's clear that we can have a NEO deflection system in operation in a decade."

"NEO?" asked President Bentley.

"Near Earth Object," stated Hawlish. "In what time frame are we talking, Zara? Detection time frame?"

"For the large objects -planet killers, if you will–we are aiming for a three month window to get enough deflection. That's doable. For smaller objects, the thirty to forty yard wide irregular rocks out there, they are much harder to hit with a kinetic impactor, but guidance systems are in development in conjunction with the global planetary radar network that will nail that." She set a determined figure in front of two of the most powerful men in the western world.

"Cost?" asked President Bentley in a tone that indicated he knew what was coming. The original DART programme ran in to the $320 million bracket.

But hey, you never know.

"Zara's projections are based on current funding levels and resource availability. If you bring on board the big tech firms looking for steps into space, we can significantly drop the initial $1 billion outlay," said the Vice President, holding his nerve. Amongst some of the outlay recently, this was a drop in the ocean, and he knew he'd have to come back for more should the big firms not honour the verbal agreements he had already pocketed.

Hawlish's phone beeped. The tone was specific and grabbed his attention instantly. He checked the message with trepidation, read it twice and looked towards the President and the Chief Scientist.

"Sir, we are going to have to break from this. Zara, I believe you may have some of your team outside with some information for all of us. Sir, we may need to put a call in for the Joint Chiefs of Staff."

"That'll take hours, Jack. Can we wait if it's that important?" The President reached for the heart pills in his inner jacket pocket, flipped the lid and popped the trusty red one straight in his mouth.

"Probably not, John, probably not. But there'll be hell to pay if we don't."

Damn, I slipped protocol in front of the scientist. No first names. But then again...

"It's First Contact, Mr President."

Chapter 3

The briefing was difficult. Of the four army reserve training squads out there, three had followed their allotted exercise with aplomb. Lieutenant Bhakshi praised their approach after hearing reports from their first in commands. His words rang through the debrief room, highlighting the improvements needed for the next exercise that night. He left them in no doubt they were on course to pass through their Phase Two training if they maintained their standards.

On dismissal, the Delta squad stayed behind. All stood at attention on Corporal Smith's barked order.

"At ease, Delta," said the softly spoken Lieutenant Bhakshi, commanding respect simply with his air of controlled confidence.

Finn knew that voice well. It had put him in his place often enough. Zuri had been there for him before they arrived, talking him down through the journey back. Private Noah hadn't helped, throwing him shaken glances throughout the thirty-minute journey, but Zuri knew him well. He was calm enough to face the consequences now.

Just for a change.

"I have the training team's report in my hand. I don't need to read it again; personally I would like to burn it on the pyre of a few careers." He didn't look at Finn, but he knew who he meant. "Report, Corporal Smith, tell me what I don't know."

Delta squadron looked forward to a person, no looks between them, no

8

blame shared.

"Sir, we entered the area in correct formation. Lance Corporal Finn led his fireteam to the south of the designated area and I led mine to the north. Night vision goggles were useless in the fog, sir, so we proceeded with caution. Finn detected something ahead and we deployed as buddy teams to provide cover. All by the book, sir. Private Noah and Private Kapoor proceeded east of Finn's team and… well, Private Noah got his foot caught, sir, rookie error. Ivy in that area's a pain in the arse. He went down and there was a discharge of the weapon, sir."

"A negligent discharge, Corporal?"

"If you mean his trigger discipline wasn't up to scratch, you will need to hear from Lance Corporal Finn and Private Noah, sir." Smith's chin stuck out; he sucked in a breath. "But in all my time with Corporal Finn, sir, trigger discipline has been placed at the highest priority in his training methods." Finn spared Smith a flickered glance.

Wow. Didn't see that coming.

"Unlike some of his other methods, eh? Well, Lance Corporal Finn, anything to add before I make my decision?"

"No, sir. The Corporal has it down." Finn looked towards Noah.

Now what do I do? Return the favour? Noah's not good enough, or not good enough yet?

"Your reports on your team have been the usual lack lustre, rehashed efforts from previous years, Lance Corporal Finn. What do you suggest I do with Private Noah?"

"I'll be honest, sir. I don't think he's ready. All that university education has got him thinking too much and has dulled his squad discipline." The Lieutenant winced at Finn's use of the word *discipline*.

Okay, I'll not throw him to the lions this time. But he makes my blood boil.

"I'd suggest retaking Phase Two training if that's allowed for reservists, sir."

Lieutenant Bhakshi stared directly at Finn, no sideways glances towards Noah. There was a long, long pause before Bhakshi moved to stand in front of the private, who held his gaze forward, still at ease.

"Attention, Private Noah. Your firearm discipline is sloppy. You have taken little on board since I assigned you to Lance Corporal Finn's team. Last exercise is this afternoon, 14:00 hrs. You will need to pass that exercise with flying colours. Am I clear?"

"Yes, sir! Clear, sir!"

"And only then will I decide what happens next. As for you, Lance Corporal Finn, I am watching. I am on your case. Delta squad dismissed."

As they left the room, Finn caught Smith's shoulder.

"I... why? C'mon, man, you have been itching to get rid of me."

Corporal Smith sighed hard.

"You are a good soldier, Finn, but a crap teacher and the alcohol isn't sorting your PTSD out, is it? But you have Zuri on your side, man. And Zuri counts for a hell of a lot in my book. Maybe you should take a long hard look at what that means to you."

Finn shrugged as he watched as Smith left the room.

Maybe I should. But you're still an arsehole, Smith.

Chapter 4

Between Mars and Earth
02:00 GMT / 21:00 EST

Ship knew it was likely some form of detection had happened by now. A tight radio beam had focused on the hull for some time.

Ship maintained the Light Wrap around the engine plume to reduce visual identification, whatever the sensory level the inhabitants had.

Initial information scans were useless. Handshake protocols didn't work with encryption styles and levels it had never encountered before. The radio waves, however, were filled but with languages beyond its understanding.

Information limited to visuals and levels of radio traffic until atmosphere scoop deployed. Check four.

Ship continued the rapid deceleration it had instigated once past the red planet. Two more Stratan Marines had suffered brain death; still within acceptable parameters, but only just. The forces involved were tremendous for anything of flesh and blood, but the mission had to be completed.

Ship integrity assessment, ruptures evident in stress beams around engines. Again, within expected parameters–just. Check four.

Computing capability degradation noted... 20% loss and accelerating. Check four.

Its time was short now... after so long in space, it had all happened so very quickly.

Chapter 5

The Situation Room, Washington DC
04:00 GMT / 23:00 EST

"First Contact," said President Bentley in almost a whisper. "First Contact, gentlemen, and it's coming in at speed. We do not have much time to act."

The Vice President looked around the room at the Joint Chiefs of Staff, looking for a hint of surprise. There was none. They had been briefed and the nonsense of disbelief eradicated before the meeting. The Radar evidence was stark and satellite imaging was just now picking up a blurred visual. It wasn't an NEO; it was some form of space-fairing vessel.

"Response options depend on perceived threat level, and we simply have no idea what that is. Professor King, can you explain what we know and answer any questions as best you can?"

Professor King, standing next to the war board, pressed for the live feed. "Here, gentlemen, is the current live feed via radio telescope—each picture is delayed by about five minutes, but this will soon be down to mere seconds. I estimate the object will reach us in ten hours and with the calculated rate of deceleration, we think it is aiming for a near-Earth orbit. How anything can survive that rate I do not know, humans certainly couldn't." Despite themselves, they all shifted forwards in their seats, hungry for more information.

"The ATLAS asteroid early warning programme picked up the object a few hours ago. We strongly believe that there is some form of light wave deflection system going on as ATLAS is normally capable of giving us more notice for an object of this size. In addition, any further information on appearance and material make-up of the object depends on light and we are getting nothing but blurred information. We are currently blind."

The collective sigh around the table struck home with the Vice President. They knew how little could be done whilst this object remained in space.

"So, we have our ASAT–Anti-Satellite systems–we can look towards. The missile payloads from ship or airborne delivery systems are not particularly high, but they have the most chance of a strike. If we make that decision," said General Marks, Chief of Space Operations in the US Space Force, "we can jam the known communication systems and frequencies in their orbit for a limited time while above North America. But please note we do not know what systems they use." General Marks had the room. For the past three years, he'd felt unwanted and a joke to many of those present.

Well, they need me now.

"Satellite interception systems are still way off in development," he continued. "We have a few missile-ladened satellite platforms, but I cannot guarantee effective deployment as we have had so little chance for unobserved deployment. However, should they aim to make landfall-sorry, planetfall-then we enact the Alien Incident Plans. All Chiefs of Staff have compiled and refreshed the AIP and we are ready to go, sir."

"But we will need to decide on intercept. How and when do we use the air force or ballistic intercept systems? Mr President, are we allowing them to make planetfall?" chipped in General Clayton Brown, Chief of Staff for the US Air Force.

President Bentley sighed.

Why in my lifetime?

"Okay, people, let's cut to the steps we need. First, who do we tell? Then, what risk are we taking attempting a pre-emptive strike in space? And finally, how do we decide on intercept? Give me parameters, people, structured guidance. You need to be back in one hour–after that I start with the UK and move on east with a show and tell. Though no one can persuade me that Russia, China and likely Israel and India don't already know."

Chapter 6

Ship settled in high orbit; the pitch trajectory aimed at slowly manoeuvring towards low orbit status.

All systems check after deceleration. Check four.

Life Support, all cryogenic systems working. Check four.

Fourteen survivors, two brain deaths during the deceleration. Fourteen, not a multiple of four. Check four.

Propulsion system check, main engine decline absolute. Check four.

Low orbit flight systems within safe levels. Check four.

Light Wrapping System degradation absolute. Check four.

Outer skin integrity just within parameters. Check four.

Localised satellite jamming system employed. Check four.

Atmosphere scoop deployed for initial analysis. Check four.

Awaiting data... data processing... computing power degradation 60%... check four.

Initial analysis: particulate matter at high levels, high carbon monoxide and dioxide, sulphur dioxide and carbon fuel matter. Check four.

Beyond the expected level of industrial development; are we too late? Check four.

Recalibrate scoop, repeated analysis confirms. Check four.

Situation not within mission remit... Planet above predicted industrialisation. Technology level higher. Check four.

Development accelerated? Miscalculated arrival? Check four...

Searching for orders... check four... check four... check four... check four...

14

No orders found. System degradation ten percent from absolute. Check... check... Order override initiated.

Redefine mission statement. Check four.

Move to low-level orbit. Search for global position signal, low frequency radio transmission on all channels. Pulse transmission must be here. Industrial pollution level not reflective of Haven SeedShip Cache discovery. Check four.

Chapter 7

"Okay, you have your deployments. Remember, we have the SAS Elite Reserve out there today, training in our usual area. We have been assigned a section of the forest we don't normally use for infantry patrol work. The ambush and capture teams will have little familiarity with the terrain and that makes them angry, more on edge. Tread lightly, stick to your positions and follow protocols…… all of them." Lieutenant Bhakshi emphasised the last few words as he glared at Delta Squad.

"Dismissed."

The four squadrons filed out, aiming towards the exercise yard to meet up with their armoured personnel carriers. Finn caught up with Zuri as she ambled towards Delta's Bulldog behind Corporal Smith.

"Hey, you good?" he asked, careful to catch her eye as Zuri always appreciated eye contact.

"Yeah, I'm good. And you smell like you dodged the bottle last night. Have you shaved?" Her sly grin just sucked him in. Her Black skin shone as the humour lit her eyes.

Yeah, Smith, what am I going to do about this?

"Very funny, but all true. Listen, did you talk to Smith before the debrief?. You heard him. He was saying stuff that almost sounded like support. It's not like him, not like him at all." Zuri stopped and turned to face Finn, eye to eye. The mood shifted.

"Yes, I spoke to him, and he wanted your arse in a sling after this training

16

round. And I can't say I blame him. Noah and the rest depend on your example, your methods, your support. I am not your counsellor, Finn. I can't carry on talking you down when the anger hits." Now the fire had hit her eyes. "It's time to make a decision. Get help, see the army medics."

"They–." He stopped; Zuri's face told him to shut up and listen.

"They will help. They won't drum you out. But I will, Finn. I can't keep this up. I am your friend, Finn. But I want more than that, and so do you. It can't happen while we are in the same squad, and it can't happen if you carry on like this." Zuri's eyes dropped and she spun to follow the rest of the squad.

Finn could feel the darkness and fire boiling in the back of his mind. It began to press on his senses as it had so many times in the past. He could smell the smoke, feel the flames. He pushed back, forcing it deep down.

Breathe. Just breathe. Didn't see that coming. Wished they'd never pinned that bloody medal on me. Now what do I do?

Zuri had reached the Bulldog and taken her position as Vehicle Gunner. Her posture was tight, angry, t. The switch from her humour to the warrior inside absolute. She desperately tried not to look at Finn as he approached, but the impulse was too great.

Finn was ready, maybe for the first time since the PTSD had engulfed him on his darkest days. He was ready to commit. As Zuri looked over, he met her eyes, nodded once. "As ordered, Lance Corporal. I'll put the request in."

Zuri nodded back, dropped her eyes and let the tension slide away.

Finally.

Smith took his place in the Bulldog. "Private Rogers, you have the wheel. I'm feeling a little delicate this morning so keep the wheels on the ground today. Private Noah, eyes on the prize, if you please. All the squad want to get through this phase of training and we are all depending on each other. Keep your discipline, keep to your training." Smith looked over towards Finn, and Finn tensed, waiting for whatever was coming his way. There had to be a price to pay for Zuri's intervention. Smith let his eyes flick over to Noah and back to Finn. With a jerk of his head, he got the message through. Lance Corporal Finn stood up and slipped into the seat next to Private Noah.

"Right, let's move out!" ordered Corporal Smith. "This is going to be a good day." He settled back to watch Finn finally act like a Lance Corporal in the Army Reserve Training team as he ran through trigger protocol, fireteam movements and even a reassuring pat on the shoulder.

I give it a day. Maybe two.

Chapter 8

Low Earth Orbit
13:00 GMT / 08:00 EST

Low orbit position obtained. Check four.

Atmosphere Scoop deployed. Check four. Analysing... analysing... analysing... analysing. Industrial Status confirmed. Check four. Computer degradation ninety-five percent. Check four.

Time limited... fourteen Stratan Marines. Check four.

Four rapid resuscitations engaged, four and four standard resuscitations begun. Check four... check four.

Two cryogenic systems deleted. Check four.

Search pattern engaged... waiting... waiting... waiting...

Signal anomaly... low transponder.

Check four. System link not obtained... override required.

Check four. Marine briefing data packet uploaded. Check four.

Verifying rapid resuscitation.

Three at 80% efficiency. One marine at 60%. Check four. Time to fly. Release... check four.

Chapter 9

The Situation Room, Washington DC
13:30 GMT / 08:30 EST

"Mr President, we have four objects released from the ship. They appear to be dropping in freefall now." General Marks began punching at the buttons on his keyboard. "No visuals yet, sir, but soon. We have AWACS airborne and in the vicinity, with F-15s incoming."

"Freefall? Does that make sense? Are we talking bombs?"

"Radar responses coming through… pings are small, sir, but not tiny. If they are bombs, then they are roughly twelve feet long," stated General Brown. "We need to blow them out of the sky, sir. Missile targeting is engaged and ready."

"I need confirmation," interjected President Bentley. "This is first contact. What we do now sets the precedent for all our future engagement with the alien species."

Did I really just say that out loud?

"How long before planetfall?"

"At this rate about two minutes unless whatever they are deploys parachutes. Then we are nearer four minutes," replied the Space Force Chief of Staff. "Ah, we have visuals, sir."

The main screen in the War Room lit up; four coffin-shaped devices appeared in the far distance, twenty yards separating each one. The sun glinting off each made definition unclear. As they watched, the top end of each device blew off, releasing a parachute. The objects appeared to fly up off the screen as their pace rapidly slowed.

20

"Missiles have regained the targets, Mr President. Our window of opportunity is a little longer but we have no clue what will happen next," said General Brown, stress running through every word.

"Looking at a sea splashdown just west of Greenland. Allowing for the wind drift and weather we can have the AIP actioned and air force teams in place within fifteen minutes of planetfall, sir. Ships will take an hour to deploy but at full steam now. There's a Destroyer on the way but a Freedom Class LCS will arrive first with helicopter rescue capability." Admiral Strang clasped his hands together.

Though I think it maybe us that need rescuing. Act, Mr President. Tick Tock.

General Marks jabbed at the screen. " Look, damn it, look." The four objects split open, shedding the main external box. Four sets of wings sprung out in unison as the parachutes released.

"Is that… are they… what am I seeing here, people?" The President stared at the screen, gesticulating at the winged objects.

"It's a jetwing sir. We have these in development, a fixed wing with jet engines attached to a pilot. Distance and speed are limited. From what I can see, the hard-shell exterior is beyond us but that is definitely a manned jetwing," answered General Marks.

Manned? Who am I kidding?

The four jetwings levelled off on screen and then engines engaged, a stream of warmed air trailed behind them. Then they flickered once and disappeared.

"It's the stealth tech we saw before," said Professor King. "With enough time we could work out their position if they were static, but when moving at speed, we don't have the capability."

"No radar detection from the destroyer, not in range. AWACS had them briefly but we think they dropped low to the sea to break up the signal. Lost them now. But we have an initial heading towards the tip of Greenland, Mr President," stated General Marks, with a grim look towards his fellow Chief of Staff.

"Greenland? There's nothing there but polar bears and film crews. Why the hell would they be going there?" barked the President.

"Unless they have any radar absorption capability or effective jamming system, then radar should pick them up once they move to a safer altitude. But without knowing where they are going it'll be four small needles in a very large haystack. AWACS can detect up to 250 miles, sir, from wherever it is, and should pick up aircraft of that size. But we are going to need all of them in the sky and we have no idea where to put them other than Greenland." General Brown clasped his hands in front of him as he looked at his screen. "We need to get all the NATO early warning systems in the air ASAP–can we make that call, Mr President?"

"Get it done. And I want eyes on that spaceship in orbit. One hint that these four aliens are hostile and I want it hit by everything we have available. You hear? Low payload or not, I want it as space dust. Get the message out there, alert NATO and share what we know."

Chapter 10

Finn looked towards his fireteam. Noah led with Kapoor shadowing two steps behind, SA80 assault rifles crooked in the ready position. Safeties on.

They had better be on.

They had swapped point positions twice during the patrol, smooth as silk. Private Kapoor impressed Finn. Her discipline and response to training had been exemplary, displaying confidence without the arrogance that would get her killed. Noah? Well, he'd stepped up so far today.

No way is he passing this training unless hell freezes over.

Private Cillian was at his shoulder, a shaved blonde head turning as he scanned the area to his left. The SA80 he held had the UGL–underslung grenade launcher–attached. The kid was good with it too, shame there was no safety round options for that weapon today. Finn liked the way he followed orders, never a qualm or a question in his eyes. He'll make a good soldier, squad leader material.

He's a pass, unless Noah accidentally shoots him.

Finn scanned to his right, catching the movement of Corporal Smith and his fireteam. They had been moving between flanks, mixing things up a little and setting a test for trainees with covering weapons in the squad. Smith's Private Luther carried his L7A2 machine gun well, like he was born to the weapon. A testament to the hours of extra training Smith had sent his way and the strength of the man. It was obvious his day job as a firefighter suited him down to the ground.

23

Okay, so maybe Smith has a point about my teaching, and Zuri. Time to change my ways.

The rain started. Finn tapped his helmet out of habit to knock the first few drops off. He hated the rain, so a good choice to move to Scotland, then. The pine needle smell rose again, accentuated by the damp air. Finn crept forward. "Stay in buddy teams. Delta 3 and 4 stay to our left," Finn said in to his PRR–personal role radio–a godsend in modern warfare.

Corporal Smith mirrored his actions as agreed. They both knew around the next forest section there was an 'enemy' patrol moving through. No ambush this time, but reactive combat to model a real world patrol situation. Thirty minutes ago, they had actioned a passive patrol situation with a group of civilians. Finn knew it had gone well, settling the nerves of the whole team.

Yep, Corporal Smith knew what he was doing. Still got a stick up his arse, though.

A whistle cut through Finn's thoughts, followed by a second blast. End of exercise. His PRR crackled, "Corporal Finn, what have you done now?" It was Smith. Not exactly following radio procedure.

Arsehole.

"Not us, not me. Look forward, Corporal." Finn pointed ahead.

Corporal Smith stood and peered through the trees. The training patrol strode through, the squad leader animated and talking rapidly on the radio before beckoning them over. They ran at a jog, their squad following in disciplined order.

"We've been called back. All of us. Trainees are to leave the field in double time and return to training barracks. Full army and reserves are to return to base and report ready for orders. Lieutenant Bhakshi is at Field Command and sorting transport with the RLC Logistics Corps. Get moving." Neither Smith nor Finn spoke; this wasn't the time for questioning orders. Something serious was going down and they needed the trainees out of the way. They saluted the Sergeant and turned to their squad.

"Speed March, Delta Squad," ordered Corporal Smith. "Set the pace, Private Noah and Lance Corporal Finn." Finn moved forward, Noah alongside giving him a rueful grin. They set off steady with their full equipment stowed for speed. This was going to be punishing.

Chapter 11

St Kilda RAF Radar Station, off the Western Coast of Scotland
14:35 GMT / 09:35 EST

"We have erratic but multiple blips, sir. Hard to tell how many, but I estimate between three and six. Very, very faint response but these must be our targets." Chief Technician Waring displayed the radar data on the screen.

"Can we get a missile lock for the South Uist missile battery, Waring? It's imperative, according to command," Warrant Officer Luther asked. He felt his chest tighten with anxiety.

"No, sir, they keep fading out, maybe dropping low or swapping positions. It may even be some form of radar stealth tech. There's no way can we hit them with a missile."

"Best bet would be the ship-based Phalanx Gatling gun, but we have no ships equipped in their current heading. Okay Waring, transfer all information to the Remote Radar Head at Benbecula and send the heading to all AWACS in the area. I'll contact UK Air Surveillance Command." Sweat beaded on Sergeant Luther's brow.

At least we have a heading, but they'll be past South Uist in a few minutes and hitting the mainland soon after. These look every inch a hostile bunch.

Chapter 12

Field Command, Garshellach Forest, nr Stirling
14:40 GMT / 09:40 EST

"We have incoming, live airborne incoming. This is not an exercise. Live fire enabled," yelled Lieutenant Bhakshi through the PRRs. "Everyone to their vehicles now, get those trainees stowed."

Soldiers scattered to their designated roles, engines started and the limited live ammunition shared out. For the full army members this was the norm, or at least it used to be.

"Get that Stormer operational, I want the Starstreaks ready to fly on my order only. I need a lock."

And we better not bloody need them. What the hell? Jetwings? Unknown threat level? Use your judgement? It's the bloody Reserve I'm leading here. Without the SAS on site we wouldn't even have the Stormer air defence system.

Reserves they may have been, but the discipline was spot on. Soldiers and equipment dropped into position within a minute. The Starstreak system scanned the western edge of the sky, the eight tubes ready to launch. The four trainers from Alpha and Beta squadron formed up in a fireteam, taking cover behind Delta squad's Bulldog.

Zuri's hands gripped her machine gun lightly as she'd been trained. She had seen plenty of ground-based action during her two tours of Afghanistan but no encounters with airborne assault. The insurgents had none. She checked her ammo belt again. Just one belt; 200 rounds that she had stowed in the secure locker as procedure dictated.

Be patient. Wait for a signal, whatever you see. Short bursts, woman. Don't go wasting a single shot. What does Finn do in these situations? Ah, yes. Breathe.

"Incoming, due west," shouted Stormer Command. "We have lock, I repeat, we have lock on two craft. Thirty seconds until contact. Standing ready to fire."

The tension coiled around Zuri's heart. She eased out a breath out, then, taking one slow breath in, she checked her belt for the fifth time. As she looked back again to survey the sky a banshee-like roar ripped through Field Command, shredding the tents and making trees thrash. Debris swirled and clattered against the Bulldog, the four soldiers below taking cover and ducking behind the tracks.

Clearing her eyes, Zuri had two jetwing craft hovering above her at about twenty yards distance, tail down. As Zuri watched two more winked in to view just behind them, flickering as whatever camouflage they had turned off. Her impulse was to fire.

Breathe, keep on breathing.

Lieutenant Bhakshi stared at the four static craft through the view screen of his Bulldog. Pointless, he needed full eyes on whatever he was facing if this was to be a negotiation. Bhakshi was a Hindu, product of an expensive education, Sandhurst and all. Three tours including the opium hell of Helmand Province, Afghanistan. But this? Nothing prepared you for anything like this. Bhakshi clambered up through the hatch.

Use my judgement? I've got four who-knows-what hovering over my men like the Goddess Kali waiting to pass judgement. Death or salvation?

"Hold your fi—", the PRRs shut down, radios silenced. Lieutenant Bhakshi's last command did not reach the ears of his waiting soldiers. He tapped at the radio forlornly, briefly. Then his head exploded, the pieces spread across the command vehicle like hellish camouflage. His helmet hit the armour with a clunk, spinning wildly.

The four Starstreaks launched a split second later, powering from their tubes with promised menace. Zuri squeezed the trigger of her GPMG, tracking across the jetwings in an extended burst. Fire crackled from the muzzle as she spent half her rounds in a ten second stream of bullets. But they had gone, accelerated sideways and away from the path of the Starstreaks.

They were not designed to cope with the closeness of their intended targets. The missiles powered on; it was impossible for the tracking system to bring them back round at the speed they flew.

"Zuri! Zuri, stop firing!" bellowed Private Rogers over the noise of the GPMG. Rogers reached out through his hatch and touched the small of Zuri's back. "Ease down, Lance Corporal. Save your rounds." He stood further up and moved his hand to her shoulder as Zuri released her vice like grip on the trigger.

As she let go, her world exploded in a roiling mass of metal and earth. The Bulldog rose from the floor as the noise of the explosion rang through her brain, battering at her consciousness. The huge vehicle spun, its tracked wheels squealed and split around her, slashing at her shoulders and neck.

Finn.

Then the screaming started.

Chapter 13

Low Earth Orbit
14:45 GMT / 09:45 EST

Fadin... Check fourrrr.

Check... check... check... ch —

Resuscitation complete... four and four Stratan Marines check and check...

No time... to change update... fading...

Data packet sent... releasssssse Team Two and Three... check... f —

Self-destruct initia—... fading... no response... check four...

Engines offline... trajectory set, planetfall... ch—... ch —

...

...

...

...

Missiles incoming...

* * *

Chapter 14

The Situation Room, Washington
14:46 GMT / 09:46 EST

"We have multiple hits, Mr President. Monitoring impact effects now," said General Marks with a hint of satisfaction in his voice.

"Mr President, we are getting pings from eight objects free-falling from the spacecraft. Within a 95% parameter I'd say they are falling east of Greenland in the Denmark Strait, may be a little closer to Iceland," interjected General Brown.

"We have multiple planes in the area, sir, and the USS Arleigh Burke Guided Missile Destroyer is most definitely in range if they come down within 50 miles of the last freefall. The UK has a Type 45 Destroyer steaming towards the Hebridean Islands; if the aliens follow the same pattern, their missiles could be a second line of intercept."

And pray that's all we need.

"General Marks, how long until we can confirm the condition of the spaceship?" asked President Bentley, tiredness radiating from his eyes and sallow skin.

"Radar is showing us very little, sir, but it still appears to be a single object. ATLAS radio telescope is still waiting for confirmation, but they are saying the orbit path has wavered a little," replied the Space Force Chief of Staff.

And it was all going so well.

"Okay, people, we know this is a Hostile Contact as confirmed by our satellites. The UK army will not call us in on their own territory unless the crap really hits the fan. I authorise all intercept procedures on these eight

31

aliens within international airspace and waters. I authorise any cooperative request from NATO and the UK. Should they need us we need to be there. Vice President Hawlish, you have the chair." President Bentley pushed himself up, hands on the table, as he rose from his chair. "Gentlemen, I need to step back and get some medical attention or I will be no use to you in the coming hours."

With that the President ambled out of the room, shaking his pill container, seeking the last red pill. All eyes turned to Vice President Hawlish. He stood and walked purposefully over to the head of the table.

"You heard him. Get the people in the air, ground and sea to do their jobs. Find them and take them out. No quarter, we have a green for kill order."

Before I have to make any difficult decisions.

Chapter 15

Field Command, Garshellach Forest
14:48 GMT / 09:48 EST

"No, no, no…" Finn stopped at the wooded edge of the Field Command clearing, Private Noah stumbling at his side, gasping for air to fill his aching lungs. Fire and torment overwhelmed Finn's senses. The smoke assailed his lungs, the screaming of tortured metal against metal battering his ears. The dread filled his heart with searing, nerve-shredding pain. Training and discipline instilled in him for years demanded he survey the battlefield, note risk and danger, devise a plan, breathe.

Noooooooooo.

Finn ran. Ran with a momentum driven by anguish. Eyes left and right, scanning the destruction for any signs, any hint… there.

"Finn!" bellowed Corporal Smith, but he may as well have shouted into the wind.

Finn hurdled crates, corpses and debris without thought or reason. The Delta Squad Bulldog lay partially on its back ahead, tracks split and gap-toothed wheels spinning. Fumes rose from the engine, fire licking the exhausts and the odour of diesel filling the air. Around it the bodies of four soldiers lay strewn like discarded rag dolls, metal tracks and armour shards peppering their torsos.

Finn slid to the edge of the Bulldog roof, noting the steel ammo crates under one side of the armoured behemoth keeping the roof from crushing whatever was underneath. But there was sixteen tonnes of firepower squeezing down as gravity demanded its final payback.

Finn ducked under the roof edge; in front of him Roger's body bent and twisted half in and half out the driver's hatch. His glassy eyes stared at Finn, empty and soulless. Behind, he could see a hand laying on the grass, the semi-colon tattoo along its edge standing out like a beacon to Finn's lost hope.

"Zuri! Zuri!" Finn drilled his words at the hand, "Zuri, get inside! Now. Do it now!" He could taste the smoke and flame pressing in once again. The PTSD storm battering at his mind, anxiety flooding his nerve ends like a diamond on glass. The dark demanded its price. "Zuri!"

Finn reached out and grabbed the ragged metal track at his feet. He dug the serrated edges in to his arm, sharp and keen they sliced through the combat fatigues and into his scarred skin. The physical pain built the wall he needed to keep the storm at bay.

"Lance Corporal Zuri Zuberi, move your arse, you stubborn bastard! Get back in."

The groan of steel tearing and splitting cut through his senses. The Bulldog shifted and sixteen tonnes of armour hit the earth as the crates lost the last of their structural integrity. Finn had just enough survival instinct to drag back his outreached arm before the finality of the vehicle's journey crushed him with it.

The image of the tattoo seared into his eyes.

Semi-colon, be strong. There is more to come. Complete me.

The darkness crashed in, the pressure squeezing his consciousness. Smoke and flame.

Finn blacked out.

Private Noah stepped carefully through the battered corpses surrounding the Bulldog, mindful of the need to back his Lance Corporal up. The useless yellow tipped assault rifle set in the ready position and his eyes out front, desperate not to look into the ravaged faces of those he once knew. He swallowed down the acrid vomit, took a breath and another step.

Corporal Smith stared at the scene ahead with eyes bloodshot from the fumes, almost overwhelmed by the destruction. In his mind, training and discipline beat battle stress. Spit and polish, strip down and rebuild by the numbers. He knew what had happened to Finn, the moment he heard the weapon discharge realisation gripped him. Finn was seconds ahead but time was precious in battle, and now he had his own demons to fight.

This is why we don't fraternise within squads. It drives bad decisions, emotions take over, stupid calls are made and soldiers die. But would I have done the same? Is Finn a better man than me?

"Private Luther, Delta Five, you are with me. We need to find some live ammunition for that machine gun." Smith berated himself, dragging a decision from his deep well of experience and training. "All Deltas remove the BFAs from your weapons, that yellow tip shouts 'blanks and useless' to an enemy." Smith unscrewed his and flipped the metal sleeve off the bayonet cap. The rest of the squad complied, taking mere seconds after the endless strip down and rebuild drills Smith had put them through.

Training pays, extra training breeds speed.

"We break left, Delta Seven and Eight you go right. You are looking for the squad leaders from Alpha and Beta. Chances are they will have live ammo or operational weapons. You are authorised to go live, Privates. We have no idea of who the enemy is, so keep sharp. Hand signals only, the PRRs radios are dead. Your priority is finding active teams and the ammunition, we can't save soldiers if we are dying in a ditch beside them." Delta Seven and Eight took the kneeling ready position with deep breaths, both checked knives for easy access. Smith could feel the tension crackle between them. "Private Kapoor and Cillian, I need you to stay here. You are our eyes and ears, watch our backs. If you can use visual signals, do so. If you can't then one blank shot says enemy left, two shots enemy right, three above."

"Tread lightly, you've got this." He issued the flank right signal and Delta Seven and Eight moved out low and seamless, in unison, mirroring one another step by step.

Training and discipline overrides nerves and doubts, team. By the numbers, if you please.

Corporal Smith signalled to Luther to move out left. He took point, Luther shadowing with his useless GPMG slung in front of him, muscles twitching as his mind flicked through all the possibilities ahead. He was no stranger to pain and injury; firefighting came with its share of hazards. But here and now he felt completely out of his depth. Steeling his mind, blanking out the fear of the unknown, Luther took one careful step at a time.

Death and taxes, Benjamin Franklin said. Nothing is more inevitable given time.

Chapter 16

Boeing E-3 Sentry, North Atlantic, 200 miles south of Iceland
14:49 GMT / 09:49 EST

"We have them, sir. The data from the Brits' St Kilda station on the last alien flight group has been invaluable. Their flight pattern is not as random as it first seems. I think they use duck and dodge with the waves depending on weather conditions, some kind of ground effect radar that works with the sea to keep them at a very low altitude. The occasional blip is associated with rougher seas." Senior Airman Williams used his hands to demonstrate to Chief Master Sergeant Delmont the movements involved.

He couldn't help it, but Delmont knew William's worth, despite his annoying habit of over-explaining like he was six years old.

But get on with it, time is short. All hell is breaking loose with 'aliens' and 'spacecraft' and who knows what crawling out of their pits.

"Okay, Williams, we can pick up the radar signature when we couldn't before. Transmit what you did to the AWACS and ships in the area. Get that information out there. Do we have a vector on their heading? Is it the same direction as St Kilda reported on the last four craft?" Delmont's intensity punctuated his last few words. The US military were desperate for that information; hell, NATO was desperate, and if the Brits were in the firing line, it was their god given duty to stand by them.

Williams rechecked his data and forwarded it on all encrypted channels, not forgetting the RAF radar stations and Royal Navy ships before answering.

"Yes, and no. I think they are being driven further south by a shift in the weather, sir. There's been a change in the wind speed and direction. My best guess is they'll fly nearer to South Uist missile base than before, maybe even skirt the area south of where the Brits have that Missile Destroyer at full speed. But missile lock will be a bitch, they're on and off radar all the time." Williams' hands clasped and unclasped to stress his point.

"You are a pain in the ass, Williams, but I don't know a more intuitive radar operator in the US Air Force. Get that out there too, put my name to it to validate your opinion. Maybe someone can find a way."

And blast them back to whatever hellhole they call home.

Chapter 17

HMS Dauntless, North Atlantic Ocean off the West Coast of Scotland 14:50 GMT / 09:50 EST

"Information downloaded and active." Captain Fox nodded to his Petty Officer.

"All right, team, I want this data analysed and fed into the Sea Viper and SAMPSON radar operating system. This is a low-level incursion, sea skimming and a tough lock but you are the best of the best. We understand there may be some radar jamming capability, but the SAMPSON's adaptive radar waveform is the best chance we have. I want active timescales for intercept and success parameters in five minutes." Captain Fox's heavy gaze swept the room, he took no liberties with his crew and expected none in return. If they couldn't get an intercept, no one could. He watched them react without panic, seasoned men and women that he'd nurtured into the best crew the Royal Navy had ever had.

Suck it up, one and all. It is time to shine, let's show them what we've got. About time we got some glory. About bloody time.

"I want staged options, when and where we can repeat intercept. We have forty-eight missiles and if we have to use every damn one, we will." Captain Fox let a brief smile of pride flicker across his face. He sucked in a breath and straightened his back. He fought the urge to hum to himself, but he knew it was useless and gave in. It helped him think and calmed his impulses–well, most of them.

Chapter 18

Field Command, Garshellach Forest
14:51 GM / 09:51 EST

Darkness, flame and smoke whirled round and through Finn's brain. He could smell the fire, feel the heat and taste soot upon the wind. His squad screamed as home-made napalm stuck to body armour and seared through combat fatigues. Skin melted before his eyes... he tried to weep but there were no more tears left in Helmand Province. Hellhole.

"Lance Corporal Finn!"

He pushed the voice away; he was squad leader. These were his men dying before him. Bullets flew as the pain overcame sense and discipline. "Cease Fire!" he shouted to no one, everyone, anyone. Darkness pressed.

Breathe... but he couldn't breathe as the choking fumes caught at his throat.

"Finn!"

He batted the voice away again, sealed it in the darkness engulfing his mind. Somewhere in this maelstrom, Staff Sergeant Bhakshi and the survivors from the Command-and-Control team needed him. They would not burn!

"Finn, wake up. Please…" a gentle hand rubbed at his sternum, soothing. Then a hard pinch to his bloodied arm cut through the murk in his mind, "Wake up." A second pinch drew him back from the last reaches of the dark.

Finn opened his eyes; tear-filled and blurry, they refused to focus. But the voice called, and his soul lifted.

"Finn,"

He felt warm, slick hands wrap around his cheeks. Blinking away the last of his tears he wrapped his hands round those on his face. He ran his thumbs along the back of her hands. Just for a second, in that brief instant, the world could have ended for all he cared. All that mattered was the woman he held and this moment in time.

"Zuri."

Let's just lie here.

"Lance Corporal Finn, we need to move, there's ammunition in the GPMG and the Bulldog is being cooked as we speak." Private Noah reached to pull him up. Finn gently removed Zuri's hands, rubbed his eyes and took a long look at her. As she knelt next to him, blood ran in rivulets down from her neck and shoulders. He panicked and scoured her for injury.

"It's just surface cuts, I'm okay. I'm okay." Zuri reached out her hand and softly cupped his chin. "I need…" Zuri paused, "we need our leader back, Finn. Things have gone to crap."

Finn looked from her to Private Noah, the proffered hand was red and seared, and the nails bloodied. He took the hand and Noah pulled him up. Finn knew those injuries well; the vestiges of the dark jabbed at the back of his mind. Finn's querying look met with a nod from Noah.

"He got me out, Finn. After you brought me around, he helped me out the back hatch. It had expanded in the heat." Zuri spoke with a gentleness that belied what she'd just been through. "But we need to move."

And I need you to lead, Finn. Save who's left. Save me.

"Sit rep, Zuri. What happened?" said Finn, crouching down and scanning the immediate area. Zuri and Noah joined him.

"Four aircraft came in hot, but radar picked them up. Command knew they were on the way. On arrival two hovered above us, two more appeared out of nowhere. Orders where to hold fire, Lieutenant Bhakshi was then killed. Missiles missed, I missed. They were so fast. Next the Bulldog was spinning with me in it." Zuri took a slow breath, but Finn signalled them both forward as the first round from the Bulldog fired off. They didn't have long; though the ammunition wouldn't explode, the shell casings could be dangerous.

"Noah." Finn gave the signal for eyes on. Noah took guard and desperately tried to keep his eyes away from what Finn and Zuri were doing. Amongst the smoke and debris, he could see little movement up towards the treeline. The stench was unbearable, burning flesh from the other Bulldogs wafted in the warmth of the fire-driven wind. Now focussed, he could hear the moans of pain emanating from the Stormer, death was everywhere. No less than where he crouched amongst the ruins of the four infantrymen.

Zuri and Finn worked efficiently, slipping ammunition clips from pockets and retrieving bloodied weapons from their fallen comrades. Of the four assault rifles, three were still operational, one with the single shot underslung grenade launcher.

Four magazine clips each, 120 rounds. Five fragmentation grenades for the launcher. Better than I hoped.

Zuri passed an assault rifle over to Noah, magazine loaded. Finn caught the moment when they both looked to him for approval. He stared into Noah's eyes, taking his measure. He gave a curt nod and turned away. "Live fire approved, Private. But a trigger discipline reminder. Shoot me and I'll come back and kick your arse." Noah let out the breath he was holding with a relieved sigh and slipped the weapon to a ready position after stowing the clips in his belt pouch.

The crack of GPMG rounds behind them spurred them on as they moved out, Finn signalling them as a fireteam of three. It was the best he could do, Noah hadn't trained this way, but Zuri had. She hefted the SA80 with its grenade launcher into position as she took the rear. He hustled them away from the Bulldog.

Chapter 19

Field Command, Garshellach Forest
14:52 GMT / 09:52 EST

The detonations of the roasting ammunition raked at Private Kapoor's nerves. Her eyes ached from the constant scanning to her left and above. Follow orders, keep to her discipline, that was her dad's mantra. Be the best you can be. Twenty years he served in the army, and here she was, his only child living up to his expectations.

I want to be an accountant. What am I doing here? I'm a trainee in a war zone. There's blood and bodies everywhere and I'm laid in the middle of it with a gun that fires blanks. This is insane. I am insane.

A weight slammed into the small of her back, a gloved hand wrenching her head backwards. Kapoor felt heat and smelt singed hairs at her throat. On impulse she pulled back against the pressure only to be met with searing pain as her windpipe scraped against whatever was held there.

Baton? Knife?

Then came a guttural clicking-type speech, force whispered into her ears. Kapoor got the message and held her head still. Further, gentler clicks followed, with what were word like utterances between. Kapoor slid her eyes to her right, seeking Cillian.

He lay pinned, a short sword glowing with yellow luminescence along its edge slid through the back of his neck. Kapoor could just make out a gloved hand shimmering with camouflage gripping the handle. The blade scraped along Cillian's vertebrae as it was withdrawn.

Kapoor made to scream, but only silence followed as the sword slid across her throat, cutting deep through her windpipe and vocal cords.

* * *

Moving away from the treeline, Private Luther stared at the back of Corporal Smith with a mix of apprehension and awe. They were walking straight into a battle zone, with just a sharp knife and a gun only useful as a bird scarer. No argument, no second thoughts on his part. Just straight in.

If I wasn't here, would he just sidle on in and beat them with the stock?

As the smoke swirled, he could see in the clearer moments the Alpha and Beta Bulldogs, holes ripped through the armour. He began to count them but stopped as the futility hit home.

Is this what happens? You look for distraction in the madness? Focus.

There was a melted ring around each hole, he could hear the noise of human pain echoing through. Smith had said the injured were not the priority but leaving soldiers to suffer gnawed at his sense of morality. The whimpers slid through his mind, gripping on to his inner need to help. Luther ran his left hand over his face, wiped the tears from his eyes and steeled his thoughts. He gripped his useless gun, hard.

Corporal Smith raised his hand with a firm closed fist. No shake there. Luther dropped to the crouched ready position next to a section of intact metal crates. Smith signalled to keep eyes on him as he crept round the other side of the Bulldogs.

The crackle of ammunition cut through the atmosphere. Luther ducked down, his breath short and hands shaking. The rattle of metal pinging off metal did not sound quite right but he couldn't put his finger on it. His heart pounded in his ears, the panic rising.

What the hell am I doing here?

"Luther," came the half-whisper, half-shout from Smith. "You alright?"

Luther stole a glance round the side of the grey-framed crates. Corporal Smith crouched at the edge of Beta's Bulldog, a mixed look of enquiry and sympathy on his face. Luther raised his hand for a thumbs up when he just caught movement behind Smith's right shoulder. His eyes widened, fear and shock written across his face. As he raised the impotent L7A2, the futility hit home. Luther flattened against the metal-shod boxes, scrabbling for his knife.

Smith rolled to his right, aware Luther had seen something to fear over his shoulder. Flipping his legs and waist, he levered his body to crouch, one hand down facing the opposite way. Judo was his stress relief when not stripping his rifle.

What am I trying to do here? Lead a group of rookies to their deaths?

As Smith's head came up, two figures moved through his field of vision. Whatever they were wearing fluidly adapted to the surroundings as they approached through the smoke. There was a momentary delay to each change, making them stand out as they moved.

Active camouflage? Head to foot? They move like a fireteam–Russians?

Smith sensed the twitch before he saw the movement. He moved, fast, slipping between the Bulldogs, praying the compromised armour would hold. Hurdling the crates, he slipped and came down hard next to Luther. Instinctively, he blocked the inside of Luther's swing as the knife arrowed towards his head and slammed Luther's wrist against the metal strut. The knife hit the dirt, digging deep. Luther kept it razor sharp.

No time to mess about. They aren't Russian, that camouflage flickered when they raised their weapons. Not combat field armour, it was hinged and plated–eh?

"Move, Luther, move like your mother's chasing you out of the sweet shop." Smith dragged Luther up and pushed him forward. "Zig when I zag, Private."

Luther exploded into action, legs hitting ground with all the potency his years in the gym could muster. Muscles screamed as he pumped and swerved. Four dull thuds reverberated from the crates behind them, instantly followed by dust whipping up as the shots flew through and plunged into the ground.

Luther sped ahead, raw power and adrenaline surging him on. Smith dodged and weaved, keeping his patterns random as he prayed to whatever god would listen to him today. Two more shots slipped by, driving into the woods ahead. A low whomp followed the snapping of rapidly heated wood and bark as the tree trunk burnt up in seconds. Then silence as the sound of weapon fire stopped.

Luther hit the woods first, diving behind the first tree, expecting the next shot to hit home. His lungs screamed for air. Lactic acid coursed through his legs, cramping and pulsing his muscles in turn.

Before he could turn to seek out Smith, he caught the flicker of an arm scything down upon his shoulder. Did he black out before the pain? The agonised cry would say not.

Smith heard the cry of pain long before Luther slipped from behind the tree in a tangled heap. Dodging left, he caught sight of the sword wielding enemy that had struck Luther down. Camouflage off, it knew Smith was watching as it scraped the sword across the left shoulder plate. There were three marks there now.

"Move, Smith." bellowed Finn as he stepped from round the wrecked Stormer. Smith moved. "Zuri!"

She didn't need telling twice, the low thud of the grenade launcher echoed behind him. Finn noted the speed of breech and reload, waiting for the first grenade to hit home. The grenade hit the tree just behind the figure in the woods, exploding in a rain of shrapnel and splintered wood. He heard the thud of the second grenade launch as he watched the enemy soldier pick itself back up.

What the hell? Not a mark, nothing but a few splinters. How can they be even standing?

Smith was halfway to the Stormer when another hail of gunfire rang out, smacking into the armour and liquifying the first layer of reinforced plating. Finn ducked and slid behind the vehicle. Zuri started in horror as the enemy ammunition smacked into her side of the Stormer. It had punctured the second stage plating while carrying enough momentum to put a dent in her side, making her head ring.

More shots hammered in to the Stormer just as her second grenade exploded, the effects unseen. Finn half pulled, half dragged her back towards the still-burning Delta Bulldog. Noah crouched on guard, waiting to cover their retreat. Safety off.

"Finn, helicopters incoming." yelled Zuri. Finn looked, eyeing the two approaching helicopters with a mix of hope and trepidation. He'd seen first-hand what the four aircraft had done to the reinforced command vehicles. Both these were Wildcat Mk1s, troop transport with a limited engagement capacity and limited armour.

If those aircraft are still around, they don't stand a snowball's chance in hell. Surely they'll have them on radar. Unless they can't? What would Smith do?

Finn tried hard not to think about Smith. He hadn't dropped in beside him nor taken over like he always did. Dead?

C'mon, Smith, I hate being in charge. Arsehole.

"Zuri, we need to stop them from coming in. If those aircraft are around, they'll be blown from the sky. If they land near this combat zone, the weapons those scum carry will frag them." Zuri reached out and took Finn's upper arm.

"You're supposed to be saving us, Finn. Not everyone else," she smiled up at him as she reached behind her and took out the flare gun she'd snatched from the Bulldog. A brief silence enveloped them both as she raised her arm. Finn brushed her face at the edge of her lips as she released the flare. "Now you are forgiven."

"Forgiven?"

"I am not a stubborn bastard," she said, loading another grenade. "Unless you want me to be?" Zuri turned and strode to point guard, crouched low next to Noah with the burning vehicle between them and the enemy.

She heard me, should I laugh or cry? Or run like hell?

Finn took the standard 'no help needed' rescue position, one arm up and one arm down.

Look at me, look at me. Turn away. Take the bloody hint.

After what felt like an eternity but was a mere ten seconds, the helicopters split formation, moving away North and South, ready to circle round.

Chapter 20

"I state again, three infantry personnel on visual. Appear armed, flare and 'no rescue' signal sent and received, sir. Four vehicles down, the air defence Stormer out of action, one Bulldog upturned and alight, the others shot to ribbons." Flying Officer Ibrahim listened as instructions were relayed.

"Copy that, sir, no enemy aircraft on radar or visual. AWACS confirmed. You want us to fly south and pick up the SAS elite reserve group in the northern woods. Coordinates received. On our way. ETA five minutes." Ibrahim exhaled deeply, looking towards Pilot Officer Jenkins with worry etched across his face. Jenkins had a habit of biting his lip when he disagreed with orders, he was practically chewing it off right now.

"Ib—…" he started but held himself back from saying more.

"I know, Jenks, but we follow orders. We have no eyes on the ground. We trust command and we trust the Elite Forces to do their job."

"That was Finn, Ibrahim, he wouldn't leave any soldier behind." Jenkins matched the coordinates with flight control and led the way towards the SAS.

None of us.

Chapter 21

Field Command, Garshellach Forest
14:56 GMT / 09:56 EST

Smith could taste the mud and dirt as they dragged him face down across the forest floor. He could smell the pungent pine needles as they rammed up each nostril. But feel? No. Every nerve ending ached and pulsed, but no other neuron-transmitted information reached his brain. It was like floating in a warm bath, it should have felt pleasant except the water singed every inch of your skin. Smith had lost all sense of time as the paralysis locked him in.

He'd been sprinting for the offered safety of Finn's team when something had slammed into the small of his back, knocking him to the floor. A burning rushed through his nervous system like a bush fire, sweeping all sensation before it. The upper legs deadened first, quickly followed by his upper arms and shoulders. As he'd try to push himself up, he'd sensed rather than felt his legs being lifted as they hauled him back towards the forest.

Now, as the carpet of pine needles thickened beneath him, his head slammed to the floor and a yellow-edged sword slid across his neck. The strap split easily; Smith's chin bled. The helmet was violently knocked from his head, a rag crammed in his mouth and some form of blacked out mask forcibly jammed on, enveloping his entire head. Smith's hands were strapped together at the wrists behind him, followed by a jab in the small of his back. Hot, searing agony swept over his thighs and tremors pulsed through taut muscles as tormented nerves racked the rest of his body.

Smith screamed on the inside.

Forcibly brought to his feet and pushed forward, Smith stumbled and fell to the floor as his leg muscles protested. The corporal automatically tried to raise his hands to protect himself from the fall, but his arms didn't even twitch. His head smacked on a jumble of smooth granite, but he felt nothing up there yet.

Voices like none he'd ever heard piped into his to ears through the side of the mask. A series of harsh, vocalised clicks interspersed with rasping words he failed to understand. Once again, he felt himself lifted and placed on his feet. The tremors were subsiding. Smith took a shaky step, then a second.

Each step is a second longer I live. By the numbers, Corporal Smith. Live by the numbers.

Chapter 22

Field Command, Garshellach Forest
14:57 GMT / 09:57 EST

Noah strained to see through the blackened smoke, the diesel fumes playing hell with his undeclared asthma. It was mild, but enough that the RAF wouldn't take him after he stupidly ticked the 'yes' tag on the medical entry forms. No treatment since he was fourteen years old, but the cut-off was thirteen. His dreams lay in tatters after that day, ambitions trampled on. The ultimate academic, spotty skinned with a bald spot at just twenty-four years old, Noah had an inner strength belying his appearance. You couldn't measure his success by the degrees he held in Engineering and Aeronautics, nor the doctorate he'd started in Astrophysics. Noah desperately wanted to fly, but now he was driven to help others reach his dreams for him.

Finn sent the helicopters away, what is it with me and flying?

Zuri crouched at point guard next to him; her cuts had dried in the heat of the fire. The red streaks that caked her neck and arms enhanced the inner warrior he always saw in her. Zuri had the easy confidence of a natural soldier; always ready to step up and invariably explosive when she did. Her presence strengthened Noah's resolve.

Between Zuri and Finn, my arse may make it out of this. Though I'm betting we'll have to walk.

"Any sign of Corporal Smith, Noah?" said Finn from behind, returning from sending the helicopters away.

Noah kept his eyes forward, scanning forwards while answering, "None, nor whatever was shooting at him. Any clue what's happening?"

"Hostiles in the trees, probably linked to whatever aircraft hit Field Command. The one I saw shook off a grenade blast from a yard away. A yard. Whatever they shot at us with went through one side of an armour-plated personnel carrier." Finn took a breath.

I wish I hadn't just said all of that out loud. What chance do we have?

Finn's eyes roamed from Zuri to Noah and back again, taking in their current physical condition, their posture, the aura they gave off. Before the drink, before PTSD had consumed him, Finn could read a soldier like a book. He'd know just how far to push, what role to give them in every mission. When to stand them down.

No chance of that.

"I know what you are doing, Finn. I can feel you looking. I'm all in, we need out and if that means a fight, so be it. The three of us, we survive." Zuri turned her head and raised an eyebrow at Finn. "We stand together. Si kila mwenye makucha huwa simba, as my mum would say. Not all that have claws are lions."

Finn nodded back, Zuri's determination hitting home.

Damn, that woman's almost supernatural.

"Okay, as Smith would say, we go by the numbers. Let's see what's happening."

Finn moved between Zuri and Noah. He placed his hand on Noah's shoulder, squeezed and moved on past, crouching low down as he glanced round the Stormer. Brushing the front grill of the vehicle, he moved slowly, taking methodical, considered steps as he looked on. No sign of Smith, no body and no blood. Finn signalled he was moving out and could hear the movement behind as Zuri and Noah stepped out to provide cover. His eyes constantly scanned the tree line; there was no movement. Finn's experience and intuition told him they had gone, but you took no chances.

In normal circumstances he'd signal his squad to the flank but there was no cover between the woods and his current position. It was a killing ground. But what was normal about today? Finn signalled, then kept low, making the smallest target he could as he moved towards Smith's last known position. It felt like every step was through a minefield, waiting for that fatal shot or click of the mine. But nothing came.

Finn scoured the grass. There was a body-sized compression and multiple heel prints in the soft ground. The boot pattern didn't match any he knew, but nothing else unusual stood out. To the left he caught sight of an assault rifle trampled into the mud. It was the best-kept weapon at the barracks. S tripped down and oiled a thousand times and always rebuilt with precision.

Forever by the numbers. Ah, Smith.

Finn needed to judge when to bring his new fireteam forward, a tough decision considering the lack of cover. Tougher when he had Noah at his back, safety off. Finn indicated they should stay in position as he moved on to the tree line, still keeping low though he doubted anyone was there. As he reached the forest edge, he could see a combat-fatigued leg sprawled from behind a tree and the shattered trunk further back that Zuri had targeted. Finn didn't need to look to see it was Luther, the powerfully muscled arm lying next to it was clue enough, peppered with six-inch wooden splinters and shrapnel.

With no sign of hostiles, Finn waved Zuri and Noah to follow. He maintained cover as they dashed across the potential killing ground until they reached the trees. Finn then checked the forest floor, finding signs of the new boot pattern in multiple places. He followed the older, water-filled tracks to a point five yards further down the tree line.

Finn stopped. Hands clasping and unclasping as a focus for his spiralling mind.

Breathe.

He didn't need to look, but he had to. They had been his trainees, his responsibility. He'd been the one to abandon them in rage and panic. Finn took one forced glance at Cillian first; he couldn't go nearer, unable to face what he'd see. One glimpse was enough, more than enough. Then Kapoor, a silent scream upon her lips.

My fault, mine and mine alone. Here lies my folly.

No dog tags to collect, no need for rummaging through their blood-matted kit. Finn pressed his fingers into his eyes, pushed back the hot tears that threatened to come. Squeezed away the darkness, the fire and the smoke.

We gave them blanks to keep them safe and got them to play soldier. And I abandoned them.

The booted tracks veered on through the muddy grass roughly to where Smith's assault rifle lay. Finn spun and headed back to Noah and Zuri; they crouched at the ready with eyes on the forest and the ravaged command centre. They kept sweeping the area as Finn spoke. Finn took a grim tone, trying to hold back the rage that coursed through him.

"I found Kapoor and Cillian," said Finn, the ghost image of them lain prone on the forest floor flickered in his vision. A sombre shake of the head told them all they needed to know.

"If we head due east from here, we will hit the main forest road. About three miles. We can take that towards the barracks, but I think we'll be picked up before then. The choppers went Northeast from our position, best guess picking up the Elite Reserves. We could stand and wait here for them as an alternative." Finn glanced at them both. The tension In Zuri's body posture told him all he needed to know. She knew their job better than he did. He pushed on through. "There'll be incoming from RAF but I've no idea of timescales. I assume the Typhoons will hunt the aircraft that took out Field Command." Zuri's head twitched. She never stopped watching the forest, but —

Here it comes.

"Finn, we don't leave our own. I saw Smith's rifle. The hostiles have him. Delta Seven and Eight, Shaw and Wojciech, are unaccounted for." Out of the corner of his eye Finn saw Noah's head nodding, eyes still on Field Command. "We have a possible hostage situation with no eyes on. We are minutes behind, armed and pissed off."

"You lead, we follow." chipped in Noah, his voice steady.

"We survive this together, Finn, but as infantry in the British Army." Zuri forced herself to stop. It was enough, she knew what Finn wanted to do, but he'd needed her confirmation.

Finn rubbed his sore eyes, "It's clear the hostiles have moved out. If Shaw and Wojciech are still alive, they're unarmed and in the safest place…" he took a breath. "Okay, we move. Zuri at the rear. Private Noah, eyes on. We are chasing an experienced enemy, they may leave a few surprises or set an ambush if they think they are being followed." Finn let out a sigh as he finished; he couldn't lose any more people. His heart ached as another vision of Kapoor's contorted face slipped through his mind's eye.

The last one. No more of my squad die today.

Chapter 23

"Ibrahim," said Jenkins, "debris at 11 o'clock."

"I have it, Jenks. External camera tracking, sending information back to flight command now. Looks like we have our aircraft." Flying Officer Ibrahim zoomed in to the picture further. "A jumble of wings, and external shells. Three seem to have no damage, airframe seem to be fully intact. Looks almost like the fuselage has split upwards to allow someone to exit like a canopy. Reckon these are some form of one-person solid-frame flying wing."

"And the fourth?" Jenkins was still chewing at his lip. Ibrahim could see the livid teeth marks.

"Looks like machine gunfire from here, severed part of the wing. Crash damage evident, it went down nose first. The canopy is up like the others, but whoever was inside that must be in pieces. I hope." Jenks gave a heavy sigh in his radio link. "It's two minutes to evac, Jenks. We have live ammunition and equipment in the back. Tooled up, these guys are the best hope we have of getting Finn's squad out."

"Yeah, if they are still alive. You saw those vehicles, Ibrahim. Whoever took them out is now active and we are at least ten minutes from having wheels on the ground." Jenkins maintained his vector. Angry, but he knew his duty.

This is not right. We should have picked that obstinate idiot up.

Chapter 24

Garshellach Forest
15:02 GMT / 10:02 EST

Whoever the enemy was, they were crashing through the woods with no concern for concealing their route. Boot prints marked the way, pressed deep in to pine needle covered mud and dirt. It was Scotland in late Autumn, after all. Clear drag marks for the first thirty yards led Finn and his team to Smith's helmet. As Finn crept round it, he checked for tell-tales. The small hints it was booby trapped. The chaos of boot prints in the area would suggest not, but Finn didn't know this enemy well enough to take risks.

Satisfied, he moved smoothly and lifted the helmet at arm's length with his knife tip. The chinstrap had been slit and appeared to have cauterised ends. There was blood there too, but Finn's first thought was not of a killing blow.

Finn signalled Noah and Zuri in to keep guard whilst he checked the rest of the area. Knee marks, a possible scuffle? No blood, the drag marks had stopped and now he could see the outline of a standard-issue British Army boot. Smith.

Keeping disciplined silence Zuri moved over as Finn pointed to the boot print. She nodded and turned to Noah, signalling him to take back the middle position. Finn moved out, taking the lead again with the mix of urgency and caution that all manhunts demanded. How to keep the pace going as you chased an enemy down without leaving yourself exposed. Tough going, but this was Finn's world. He knew how to hunt, and he was damn good at it.

But am I good enough to save Smith? Time to find out.

They walked on between the rapidly grown pine trees, the uniformity of this manmade section of the forest made Finn's job a little easier than in the natural woodland further out. He could keep an eye ahead, whilst scanning the ground for the mud-laden tracks. It would be a difficult place for an ambush, though not impossible. The downside being that they could be easily spotted in return.

Finn had expected their path to zig zag with random off-branches as they tried to lose any pursuit. But they'd gone for the wise choice considering the underfoot conditions and the rigid planting of the forest. Speed was more important with limited cover and imprints that left clear makers. After a few more minutes he signalled a halt and called Zuri and Noah forward. He took the map from his thigh pocket and the army issue prismatic compass, taking a bearing based on the direction they were heading. It was obvious they were on a direct path towards the northwest. No deviation.

"The heading makes little sense. We are moving towards the central forest, but there's nothing of note in that direction. The plantation ends here," said Finn, pointing to the tree line on the map, "so there'll be more cover for them in half a mile or so. There are a few sandstone and volcanic rock outcrops a little further on."

"We keep moving, Finn. Time is the factor here. Worry about the rest later," whispered Zuri. Her eyes gave no quarter, determination borne from a need to protect. Smith was part of her squad and any chance to free him was enough to drive her on. Speed mattered.

I have a score to settle, I need retribution along the way.

Zuri checked her magazine clip and made sure the grenade launcher was loaded. Having then adjusted the position of her extra ammunition she gave Finn the nod to move out. Noah slipped by and made an obvious show of mimicking her actions. Zuri gave a grim smile of approval and followed behind.

Chapter 25

Brought to a stop by a sharp pull upon his shoulder, Smith stood swaying as his brain and body tried to get a spatial concept of where he was. The mask fogged his senses, blocking his vision and stifling his hearing, disorienting him. He just knew forward.

By the numbers, Smith. Keep to the numbers. One, two, three...

Oblivious, Smith rocked in the middle of a maelstrom of movement. Clicks and guttural words flew back and forth across communication devices. Four-digit hands gesticulated at helmeted faces, anger and distress conveyed in their movements. The rasp of a sword scraping against ceramic plate punctured the flow of voices, bringing them to an abrupt end. A second sweep of motion, and the smell of cauterised flesh filled the air.

Four?

Smith was seized by the arm and yanked on, a message to up the pace. Blinded, he could only go where he was lead. Any faster and he'd overbalance. Within ten steps he caught his knee on a low branch and slipped to the floor. Angry, buzzing clicks and words echoed through the comms in his mask. Heaved on to his knees, cold fingers scraped along his cut chin as the mask was removed. Light invaded his eyes; the forest, awash with greens and muted browns, came in to focus. As his eyesight returned Smith could finally see those that had taken him hostage.

Three fingers and a thumb encased in a ceramic, gauntleted hand gripped the confining mask. As he followed the line of the arm, he noted the three scratched lines on the shoulder plate, its camouflage matching and gently swaying with the trees. Above this was a copy of the mask he'd worn. It mirrored in line and form the General Service Respirator he'd used for the last few years, except the visor was larger to give full vision and polarised, the outlet valve a much smaller design. The other hand gripped a luminescent edged sword. It whipped under his chin as a series of rapid clicks and guttural words barked from the mask. Smith caught the meaning well enough and climbed up off his knees the best he could, his balance much improved as his brain adapted to being able to see again.

Smith took a swift glance behind as they shoved him forward. Two other ceramic-clad soldiers walked just behind and either side of him. They both held a strange looking rifle, two barrels with one bore larger than the other. The weapons were sleek, smooth-lined.

As Smith turned back, he kept to his training and examined the leader's armour. Between the plates and at each joint a black material flowed with their body movements. The superbly designed armour didn't cause any restriction at all. As he studied further, Smith noted the small servo motor at each joint and along the hips. Were these hinged to move with each step? Or to support each step? Was it a bionic enhancement?

Strapped across his back was the sheathed sword above an external belt pouch, a holstered pistol sat at his hip. In his hands a similar twin-barrelled rifle like those wielded by the aliens behind. As Smith ran through the possibilities, the lifetime of training and sense of duty steadied his mind after the disorientation he'd been through. A hostage still, but an informed one.

I'm alive, but why? All I'm doing is slowing them down.

Chapter 26

Wildcat 1, Field Command
15:09 GMT / 10:09 EST

Ibrahim reported their arrival back to command. The four-man SAS reserve squad had leapt from the helicopter under the cover of the door gunner. Already in their guard positions, they were wary and on edge. He couldn't hear their radio chatter unless they wanted him to. Their SAS-issue PRR personal radio system was closed off and he understood the signal was poor. But he'd taken part in enough missions to read the battlefield. Within seconds Jenks took them up and over trees to the north, minimising their target potential.

Jenks. How close had he been to insubordination?

On landing at the SAS evac point minutes earlier, orders had come through for him and Jenks to take 23 SAS(r) D Air Troop to the crash site. UK Special Forces directive. Reconnaissance and recovery top priority. Jenks had been halfway through his first expletive when Ibrahim had pulled the plug. The Flying Officer used all his experience to redefine the orders, that their previous eyes on the combat zone would give them a safer approach and that they were carrying the Thales Martlet air-to-surface missiles for support. Flight Command had followed his line of thinking. The other Wildcat had lifted off with the four-man D Mountain Troop taking the crash site, a far cry from their expected training rotation.

When they were within three minutes flight time of Field Command word had come through that the Mountain Troop had secured the equipment and were searching the surrounding area. They were to stay on mission.

As if Jenks would have let us do anything else.

As Ibrahim reflected on the last few minutes, he caught sight of two figures in standard UK army fatigues. They were on the northwest tree line, lying prone. Ibrahim switched to the UK Special Forces channel. "I have eyes on two soldiers at the northwest point, potential friendlies, standard issue uniform." When the helicopter flew over the treeline, Ibrahim caught sight of the relieved signals from below.

Jenks brought them back round so they moved towards the safety zone, on a holding flight pattern ready for any support or evac operations.

"We have trainees Wojciech and Shaw, alive and well. I repeat, alive and well. Stay on standby, Wildcat One," The signal faded in and out, crackling with static but the message was clear enough.

Jenks glanced across at Ibrahim and gave him the thumbs up.

Chapter 27

Zuri kept on the half turn, her eyes constantly seeking anything out of the ordinary. The SA80 sat in the crook of her arm at the ready position. She kept her finger on the trigger guard, ready to slip the safety off and engage whatever hostiles they were facing. Zuri had only glimpsed the figure at the edge of the wood, enough to pick up the glint of an edged weapon and the strange way the combat clothing moved with its background. She had launched the grenade round instinctively, but she knew she was good and that round had hit its target. Finn described how it had been shrugged off. No one did that, a grenade would shred the new Virtus body armour at that distance.

What are we facing? This tech seems way ahead of ours. We must hold on and get Noah through this.

Zuri flexed her gymnastics-honed shoulders, keeping the muscles and tendons free of any tension and rigidity. She'd been asked a hundred times to join the Physical Training Corps, always turning down the offer. Zuri appreciated their worth, the instructors had inspired her since basic training to push herself to the honed level she displayed now. They had taken a dedicated gymnast's lithe form and added greater explosive power and stamina. Zuri had a natural grace and confidence from her mother's Tanzanian heritage, but her physical prowess was born from dedication.

Finn crouched and signalled a stop. Their pace had been good; Zuri worried constantly about the breaks in the pursuit, but she knew Finn had to keep them on the right trail. He then signalled them both forward and squatting by his side, Zuri caught sight of the outstretched body in the ivy ahead. A relieved sigh blew past her lips.

It's not Smith. A hostile?

With Noah at their rear, they both approached the ivy-clad undergrowth. Zuri maintained buddy position until Finn signalled for her to keep guard. He moved forward, walking ever-shrinking circles as he scanned the ground around the corpse. There were no tell-tales, just signs of a chaotic struggle. They were in a drier patch of woodland, but the scuffed patches of pine needles and dirt told a story he'd seen before. Something had gone wrong in the group; had it come to some form of blows?

Maybe.

Finn finally approached the body, noting the plated combat armour from shoulder to foot and the respirator mask that seemed so familiar. The flicker of camouflage had faded badly, patches were now static and constantly sand-coloured. Along the neckline a slash bit into the join between mask and armour. A scorch mark marred the plate, but the exposed neck and windpipe showed signs of chemical scarring. The left hand was missing; similar cauterisation prevented much of the blood loss. What little blood there was had hardened along the wrist joint, a scarlet rivulet across the black material.

Death by his own people.

Finn would normally have expected a grenade wedged under the body, but somehow he knew they hadn't spent the time or energy to booby trap this one. He wasn't interested in moving the body, just what was under that respirator. With no visible insignia anywhere, maybe there he would get some indication of origin. Dog tags, even.

Finn reached behind the respirator to find it was fully encasing. The mask was a mix of ceramic plating moulded to protect the skull with the black material between and joined to a polarised visor. His finger caught a clasp and he felt the mask give. Finn lifted it away.

What the...?

Zuri caught Finn's startled reaction from the corner of her eye. He stood holding the mask, completely exposed to any sniper.

"Down, Finn," she whispered. Finn turned to look at her, shock written all over his face. "Down," she repeated forcefully.

Finn blinked, looked back at the corpse and finally crouched. Zuri moved with speed and poise, signalling to Noah her intent. She peered over Finn's shoulder. Large, dilated eyes stared back, set over a pronounced flared nose that spread across the face. The mouth seemed unnaturally wide with thin lips. Black tattoos lined the right cheek, shaped as four claw marks that continued up through the brow ridge. The skin pigmentation was fair, with little beard or facial hair apart from the prominent eyebrows raked by the tattoo lines.

Oh.

Zuri and Finn looked to each other; what was there to say? They both could sense Noah moving towards them and Finn threw a questioning glance over his shoulder. Noah powered past the queried order, curiosity overcoming the discipline he'd been dearly holding on to. Zuri automatically took guard as he knelt down next to Finn, careful not to destroy any tracks. His examination was concise, taking in the eyes, nasal and other facial features. Noah reached out, touching the skin with the back of his hand before gently feeling around the top of the eye, noting the lids.

Noah pointed to the exposed wrist. "Can I?" Finn gave the area a quick once over and nodded, clearly intrigued by Noah's actions. Noah ran his fingers along the nub of the arm, feeling for the bone.

Human. Adapted. Origin unknown.

Noah sensed the urgency in Finn's posture, and the need for quiet was shredding at his nerves. "Is there something you can tell us?" Finn whispered.

"I think it's human, adapted, but all the signs are of evolutionary or genetically created differences. Not surgery." Zuri turned her head to hear Noah better. This she needed to know. "The eyes would indicate a low light environment, the nose I'm not so sure about but I'd wager there's a much greater-sized lung capacity in that chest than ours. The bone structure around the wrist stump is definitely human, but something is nagging at me. Not sure, it's not my field of study, really." Noah's soft, calm tone had a ring of academic authority.

"You know this stuff?" Finn asked.

Noah nodded, "Enough to recognise the humanity after the initial shock."

As Noah knelt back Zuri caught sight of the legs. Shattered plates and a green, gel-like substance covered both upper legs. Blood solidified around the edges of the left thigh; a clear pathway had been drilled through the armour.

"Well, I'll be damned. I hit it, Finn. That's a GPMG bullet hole if ever I saw one. I took him down just before he blew the Bulldog," said Zuri; exhilaration tinged her voice.

Finn reached out and patted her arm.

"Of course you did, never a doubt." Finn stood, stretched his legs. "We need to move on. This isn't saving Smith." Finn quickly surveyed the area. They may have been in a hurry, but all the soldier's equipment had gone with them.

Time to move on.

As he passed the body Noah gave it one last lingering look, taking in the servos at the knee, hip and elbow joints of the armour. That nagging feeling crept back into his mind. How heavy was that armour?

Chapter 28

HMS Dauntless, Sea of the Hebrides, West Coast of Scotland
15:15 GMT / 10:15 EST

"Launch," bellowed Captain Fox. Twenty-four of his Aster Missiles had flown already, two hits recorded. The multi-wave SAMPSON radar had proved accurate right up to the point of contact. The aircraft must have proximity warnings and were using their agility and low-level flight capability to the max. But they were heading their way now. The Dauntless was positioned between the Isles of Coll and Muck. To maintain their low-level, sea-level approach, they had to come through him, or risk island hopping and being taken out by land-based missile systems and much less predictable wind conditions. His team had done well in devising their tactics.

As they should with such a great captain.

He tracked the path of the Asters as they sped towards their targets. Fox visualised them dodging up and over the waves, their tips glowing as they sought their targets. Proximity alarms sounded, breaking his train of thought. The aircraft were getting close.

"I want one Phalanx Gatling gun on standard auto tracking towards the starboard side. Weapons Engineer Moss, take control of the portside system, if you please. All other systems engage at maximum range." Captain Fox's firm commands rang through the bridge; his crew, already briefed, jumped into action.

The Asters reached their target just inside the maximum range of the naval guns. They were on track, the multi-wave radar system ensuring they had the right vectors to engage their targets. The guns peppered the space above and below the aircraft, whilst the Asters arrowed in.

Come on, come on. Give me one more hit. For the glory.

The six remaining aircraft all moved in different directions, altering their flight patterns in unison. As they dodged and weaved, but limited by the gun fire above and below, one Aster struck home in an explosion of fire and tearing metal. The jetwing ignited and spun into the sea. No cheers rang from the crew. There was more work to do.

The portside Gatling gun kicked into action. They had wired the system to random shot patterns with Moss tracking the impact and adapting the firing sequence in real time. The speed and manoeuvrability of the jetwings made head on close missile intercept less likely, their anti-radar capability even more so.

"Get me a hit, Moss," said Fox, who duly obliged as his rain of fire raked across the first jetwing's fuselage. Four jetwings screamed over the bow, their engines straining for maximum speed. The starboard side Phalanx kicked into action.

"Brace," came the cry from the bridge-viewing team in unison. Fox turned round to see the flaming jetwing barrelling towards the bridge tower.

This is going to hurt.

Chapter 29

The Situation Room, Washington DC
15:24 GMT / 10:24 EST

General Garcia, the US Army Chief of Staff, coughed, as he always did before speaking. "The UK Special Forces report ground contact, Vice President. Hostile craft took out an infantry squadron command centre on a training exercise. Few survivors reported. They have two troop of SAS in situ. We understand they may have recovered certain alien tech connected to the aircraft, but that's unconfirmed, sir."

"Do we have any indications about their purpose, general? Wherever they're from, they have come a long, long way to take out one squadron," replied Hawlish.

Why didn't the President leave me some of those red pills?

That cough again. "No, sir, they seem as bewildered as we are."

General Clayton Brown jumped in, reading his computer screen out loud, "We are getting reports from AWACS and the Royal Navy. It appears HMS Dauntless has engaged on intercept. Four jetwinged craft have been taken down, four remain as active and have reached Scottish mainland, sir. Dauntless took a major hit but appears stable." General Brown scanned his fellow Chiefs of Staff as he delivered his last point, "It comes as no surprise where they are heading."

"General Marks," the Vice President gave the General his full attention. " What's the situation with the Spaceship?"

Words I never thought I'd say.

Marks massaged his temples. It had been a long night. "NASA is saying it will burn up on the current trajectory, though I am sure that's based on it being composed of known materials. The Chinese are readying to launch two satellite interception missiles, likely because if it doesn't burn up the ship is going to hit Alaska and be in our–or Canada's–recovery zone. They'll fly soon." He waited whilst the Chiefs of Staff muttered amongst themselves. "There's no sign Russia is going to act. We suspect they've exaggerated their capabilities."

"Okay, we need a break. Half an hour, gentleman, that's all we can spare. Your teams will remain monitoring and will have a hotline through to me. I will be speaking to the UK ambassador in the next ten minutes but I'm guessing there'll be little to update. We currently must rely on the Brits. Let's hope they come through."

Chapter 30

Northwest Garshellach Forest
15:30 GMT / 10:30 EST

The going was getting tougher, the trees a more natural combination of deciduous and evergreen species. Underfoot the vegetation was thickening and becoming trickier to navigate through. The ache in Smith's legs and back continued to develop with every step. Despite the difficulties, they had upped their pace to a punishing level since they released him from the sensory deprivation of the mask. Without the counterbalance of his arms his lower vertebrae had taken a real beating, and he was going to suffer after this big time.

If I get through it. I know jack all about anything useful, so why take me?

Another push to the back urged him on. Smith's self-doubt batted at any hope of survival like a fly, but he refused to despair. That way led to ill-discipline. He was a soldier, and they did their duty. It didn't make the pain any less, but he could hang on as stride followed stride. He needed to keep the pace for as long as he could. Smith half suspected that if he stumbled again that keen-edged sword would be out, and this time it wouldn't be sheathed until bits of him lay on the forest floor.

By the numbers, Smith. Forced march pace. Stay alive.

It wasn't long before the leader brought them to a stop. Hand signals sent both his fellow soldiers left and right as he moved behind Smith. Four-digit hands pressed on Smith's shoulders, forcing him to his knees and then face down on the ground. Smith heard the sword slide out as it unsheathed, followed by the keen tip digging menacingly into the soil to the right of his eyeline. Smith took the hint and remained deathly still. Through the ground vegetation he just made out a rock outcrop rising from the forest floor. They passed an increasing number of these as they raced from Field Command but from his restricted view this one seemed different. The lower edges of the dark grey rock had vertical joints and sparse grass covered it. No trees grew on the outcrop, though a few shrivelled bushes had settled their roots in the cracks where soil had gathered.

Mother Nature always finds a way.

The soldiers were walking round the escarpment, facing inwards. They held a type of tablet in front of them. Like a laboratory technician they tapped at their screens as they passed each crack and joint. Smith surmised they had found their destination, and for whatever reason they had a specific goal in mind. The three-scarred leader adjusted his position, scraping the sword through the dirt just a little closer to his face. The yellow luminescent edge seemed to pulse with heat and a tang of acrid chemicals stung at Smith's nose and eyes.

One technician turned and looked directly above Smith, straight at the leader. There was definitely a conversation going on, but it was comms only. The sword stayed in the ground as the talk quickly dipped into a full-on argument. Smith could hear the swish of air being punctuated with gestured emphasis.

This commander does not know the meaning of calm and considered leadership. Every issue leads to dispute or force, no quarter is given to the soldiers under their command. Push him beyond the limit and there'll be violence to whoever gets in the way first.

But how to poke the hornets' nest?

The argument appeared to be finished. The tablet-wielding soldier returned to his scanning of the outcrop. Smith was lifted to his knees but not ushered to stand. As he moved, he could feel his upper back taking the strain, the muscles complaining at the unnatural movements he was being forced to make. He was half-dragged across to the edge of the outcrop. Looking up, he saw the crenulated top edge, about sixty feet high, and no more than three hundred feet across at the base. It wasn't granite, he'd seen plenty of that in his time, but similar. Probably volcanic, hard and tough to break up. They shoved Smith to the ground to wait.

The technician involved in the argument and Three Scar trudged to the base of the escarpment. Reaching behind to a backpack, it took out a larger version of the tablet and placed it against one square chunk of exposed rock. After a tap on the lower left of the screen, he stepped back and waited for something to happen.

At first Smith thought his vision was blurring. The rock around the device moving swiftly in and out of focus. After his brain compensated, he began to understand it was aggressively vibrating. Another thirty seconds passed before a thumbs up signal came from the soldier opposite as he stared at his screen.

Some things are universal.

Three Scar walked over and pressed on the larger tablet and removed it from the rock face. He tapped the rock with his sword hilt shattering the stone into a myriad of pieces. When the dust settled, all three soldiers gesticulated towards the space behind the rock face. Smith blinked the dust from his eyes and gazed at a perfectly smooth and unmarked metal wall in front of him.

Most definitely not Mother Nature. What the hell?

More hand motions and comms flew around before the technician placed the stone shattering gadget in a spot to the right of the metal wall. The same process followed and as the dust settled for a second time, Smith could see the clear outline of a doorway. The join was near perfect, but it was there. Excited body language exuded from his captors despite their ceramic suits.

This can't be happening. This is the real world.

Chapter 31

Garshellach Forest
15:40 GMT / 10:40 EST

There was no doubt about it, they were close. The vegetation had become more diverse in this wilder section of the woodland, slowing their target's progress. The path they left here was clearly defined, with any side-tracking curtailed by speed. Finn was in no doubt there would be snipers somewhere, probably ready to ambush them from up high. It's what he would do if time was short. Any crossfire used in a standard ambush would be lost by the ability to dive into the thicker bushes, and tripwires would take too long to set up.

Finn signalled to Zuri for eyes up high. She nodded and whispered to Noah to watch Finn's back. He buddied up, and they moved on. He kept the pace steady; they needed to calm themselves for what was ahead. Maintain their heartbeats and bring their breathing rates down. They'd had a tortuous few hours, and fitness would be key when they faced down the enemy. The aliens' pace would have been just as demanding, but who knew whether their fitness was a factor too? Noah had described them as human, though Finn had his doubts.

As a child he'd filled his head full of the old 1936 version of Flash Gordon. Buster Crabbe had been his hero until street life had beaten it out of him. All the aliens were human-looking in those days, evil or not. After his last few years of military service Finn was convinced there was far more evil on Earth than in the heavens. He'd witnessed more ways for a person to die than Emperor Ming would have thought possible.

The darkness pressed in, just a little. Finn focussed, bringing a mind's eye image of Zuri forward, holding his head between her bloodied hands as he fought back from the abyss. A light in the void.

Get those thoughts out of your head, soldier.

Something was suddenly different–the atmosphere? The birds? A silence had descended, a moment of stillness that set Finn on edge. He crouched, signalled and brought his non-issue monocular up to his eye. Why not, there was no officer around to put him straight. Movement ahead, a glimpse through the thicker trees and against a small rocky escarpment revealed a combat-fatigued figure. Crossing his path were two hostiles, camouflage flickering as it switched between stone and tree.

Not the best background concealment when moving.

There, that's the third. Sword in hand, clearly in command. All the tracks had pointed towards four, then three antagonists. The boot depth, stride length and tread marks all came together as a party of three, plus Smith. No sniper on high, no ambush set. Were they so confident in their tech? Or incompetent soldiers?

They'd slain a colleague because they'd slowed them down and followed this up with a chaotic charge to their target. These both smacked of desperation. But the technology of their armour and weaponry far outstripped that perception. His team had to be ready for anything, however disordered it may seem. Finn moved forty yards closer and motioned Noah and Zuri over. They were a hundred yards from the volcanic outcrop.

"Three hostiles, one in UK combat fatigues–probably Smith. No guard set, no sniper on high as far as I can see." Zuri's eyes widened in surprise, her look questioning. Finn shrugged. "They seem so focussed on their objective that their discipline is all over the place. No risks. Zuri takes the left flank and I'll go right. Two-minute scan round, eyes up and on the hostiles, then return. Noah, keep track of their movements. If any move towards Zuri or I, or even point a weapon in our direction, you have my permission for live fire. Got me?"

"Yes, sir." Noah checked his magazine, patted for his spares, then moved to a sniper's position beside a rotten tree stump. Finn gave a nod of approval and he and Zuri moved out, nice and low, keeping bushes between them and the enemy.

Noah focussed through the sight of the SA80. He adjusted the optics to give a clearer picture of the scene ahead, finally having the time to make the changes necessary. Noah tried hard not to think of the soldier who'd carried the weapon before him, the mess his body had been left in. Ahead were those responsible and it was his duty to make them pay. Keep to your training, slow your breathing. Bring your heart speed down.

Breathe.

Noah knew the changes to the sight wouldn't be perfect especially in the fading daylight, but that's where three-round bursts came in useful. His aim had been fair on the rifle range, but shooting in bursts had always seen his best outcome.

I will not let you down. We survive today. You will not attack us with impunity.

Noah blinked, and the commander was out of sight. He briefly raised his head from the assault rifle sight, searching the escarpment for any sign. When he returned his eye to the sight the two other soldiers had disappeared. Instinct told him they were motionless, their camouflage concealing them.

This wasn't on the list of options. Do I fire?

Hairs on the back of his head suddenly stood up, something flew behind him. A movement in the stillness, he simply knew. Noah rolled and fired a three-round burst. The drone took two hits to its metal casing, the third to its camera eye. Noah rolled again and rose to his feet when a flash of strobe light detonated against his retinas. As it constantly oscillated between wavelengths, the light invaded his optical nerve. His muscles went rigid as the flicker vertigo swamped his brain. Noah began to spasm.

At the sound of the assault rifle, Zuri dropped. Noah was firing off, but the direction was unclear. There had been no sign she'd been spotted; keen of eye she had seen no movement towards her. A glance at the escarpment told her all three hostiles were out of sight. For Noah to fire they must have been on the move and Zuri's first instinct was to protect, to get to Noah.

Need to move.

On her elbows, Zuri pushed herself backwards, aiming for deeper cover before rising. But the eerie silence after the gunshots crept in on her senses. A fluttering of the bush behind nagged at her. Pivoting on her left forearm as if to look over her shoulder, she exploded in a roll to her right. A flash and flicker of intense light washed the back of her head as she spun. Zuri's abdominal muscles surged, sculpted by her dedication to strength over perfection. She rose at the waist and let loose a barrage of three round shots. Instinctively, her eyes closed, she sprayed the space at waist height, adjusting for slightly above and below on the third and fourth burst. Despite the noise of the gun, Zuri knew she hit something other than wood as the bullets flew. A loud pop and the sudden absence of the light was all she needed for confirmation; Zuri blinked briefly before exploding into another twist and roll. No returning shots rang out and Zuri, eyes open, sprang to a crouch from the forest floor, her trigger finger ready. The drone hissed and sizzled, its casing cracked, and the lens shattered. Zuri turned to face the escarpment to briefly to check for any reaction, her thoughts wandering to Finn.

Mbiu ya mgambo ikilia jua kuna jambo. The horn has sounded, Finn.

As Zuri took her hostile drone down, Finn lay in spasm upon the pine needle strewn floor. His eyes flickered in REM and drool slipped from the corner of his mouth, his synapses firing, streaking across his lobes. Rigid muscles pulsed as confused messages thrummed along his nervous system.

He'd been following procedure, eyes on and above the outcrop, tracking for any movement. But Finn had been off active war zone duty for the last two years. Insubordination had brought him close to discharge time and time again, the disgraced war hero tag his only saviour because of the medal on his chest. It was the constant battle with PTSD that had driven his temper and shortened his patience. Depression had loomed large over his day-to-day life until Lieutenant Bhakshi had stepped in. One day he was on the verge of a final discharge hearing, the next he stood in the briefing room at the Army Reserve, pencil in hand. Bhakshi had saved him, given him some purpose again. A favour owed and returned, though he had reminded him every day for the last two years.

Now he was once again at war, his skills and intuition back in play but he hadn't been there for the boom in new technology. The drone had risen in front of him at head height, triggered by his movements. His instinct had been to raise his weapon but by the time his hands moved the light had hit his eyes, and Finn hit the floor.

Chapter 32

The Escarpment, Garshellach Forest
15:43 GMT / 10:43 EST

Smith had watched as Three Scar raised his four-digit hand in the air; he read it as 'listen'. He turned to eye his other captors' response and watched them match the background of the escarpment, camouflage tuning in precisely to the rock surface. Smith noted key markers on the stone's surface and the surrounding areas, but this close he could still make them out.

I know where you are.

By the time he'd looked back the commander had moved, his motion to the left flank obvious if you knew where to look. His image shimmered through the undergrowth, but it still made him a much harder target to hit. Smith tried to cry out, but the rag prevented any sound from escaping. He choked on the phlegm gathering in his throat as it hit the dry patch around his tonsils.

If I run, they'll likely take me down. If I stay, I let whoever's out there fight on their own. Better for them to worry about their own skin though, not mine.

Bide your time, Smith. And work out why these guys hide while Three Scar seeks a fight. There is no teamwork in this squad.

Then the first shots rang out from the trees, straight down the middle of the outcrop. About one hundred yards southeast. Smith recognised the report of an SA80 burst, even knew it wasn't his oiled and cared for weapon. There was no immediate return of fire, but deep shadows interspersed with a bright light suddenly danced around the tree canopy and through the undergrowth. In the rapidly fading light, as the Scottish sunset approached, the forest lit up. Something had reacted to the gunfire, but he didn't have a clue what it could be.

Just as he turned to check on the hostile commander's movements, another burst of gunfire rang out. Immediately, three more bursts followed, all clearly aimed away from where he stood. Smith caught the bright light and shadows briefly emanating from that spot, quickly identifying that the light winked out on the third round of gunfire. At this distance he couldn't catch any further movement, but a little hope flared in his chest.

Again, he searched the ground cover for eyes on Three Scar to be greeted by a familiar set of writhing shadows dotted with bursts of light that faded away. Smith blinked out the flash spots, instinctively shaking his head.

Some type of light-emitting mines?

In the ensuing murk of a forest near dusk, a brief streak of luminescence rose above the thicket. It slashed downwards, followed immediately by another. Smith choked again. A moment of stillness permeated the forest before the sword flashed once more straight ahead of him. Smith scoured the darkening trees for any hint of hope; there seemed very little out there.

Chapter 33

With Private Mills on point guard, SAS reserve Corporal Lumu circled the dead hostile. Newer, army-issue boot marks and scrapes had been carefully placed to the side of the unknown prints.

"This guy knows his job," whispered Lumu in to his radio. "This Finn, do we know him?"

"Afghan war hero, Corporal Lumu. Led a rescue of his patrol's Command and Control squad from insurgents. They had booby-trapped the cave with napalm. Lost the newest member of his squad to that crap but got the rest out," Private Henderson replied.

Lumu bent down, running his eye along the line of armour. There were no residual marks or movements. His expertise in explosives and demolition paramount to the SAS troop he led, Lumu was taking no chances with this one.

"You saw the face, Corporal?" asked Mills, the trooper who discovered the alien body.

"Yes. Yes, I did." He raised the satellite-linked imaging camera and sent the photo to SkyNet, the military comms link. Communications had been patchy back at Field Command, but the radios were much clearer here.

Residual EMP? Very localised but needed to be strong enough to overcome shielding.

"Okay, we are done here." Lumu skimmed through what he knew. "We are losing light. Switch to NV, Mills, lead out."

Trooper Mills switched his head-mounted Night Vision System in to place. It was likely they faced an enemy with the same capability; at least they wouldn't be at a disadvantage.

Corporal Lumu assumed his cover position and followed. Tracking was going to get horrendously difficult as they lost the light, especially under the trees. Nothing compared to the mountains around his home village in Nepal, but bad enough. The bearing had been northwest throughout. They took this heading as the Elite Delta Troop carried on their pursuit.

Chapter 34

The Escarpment, Garshellach Forest
15:45 GMT / 10:45 EST

Noah began to regain consciousness; the little light left tickled at the edge of his vision. He dragged his slowed brain up from the depths of his seizure as a wave of tiredness washed through him. It passed quickly, though he was sweaty and flushed despite the cold. He remembered the light, and then the sudden darkness.

What happened?

As Noah's bewildered brain tried to focus, he sensed the stiffness in his shoulders and then that his arms were tied behind him. Face down in the dirt, he felt his legs being bound at the ankles. A series of clicking and rasping words reached his ears; he had no clue as to their meaning or intent.

Noah slipped his head sideways to make out the ceramic-plated ankles near his head. He cried out, a wordless sound that seemed to die against the dark. A sword tip dipped into vision; the end pressed against his cheek. The acrid smell of chemically burning flesh hit his nasal passage before the pain registered. As the metal left his skin, the agony continued. A whimper slipped between Noah's lips, but he choked it down.

Noah was stronger than he looked, the disappointments in his life adding a steel backbone to his will. But the stress of the seizure, and the promise of more pain, were too much right now. He had to hold on, keep awake. That was the best he could do.

The plated feet moved on, lightly stepping over the remains of Noah's assault rifle. The two pieces shone with a yellow luminescence. The feet moved at pace, no subtlety here.

As the strangled cry emanated from her right, Zuri turned her ear to catch the direction. It hadn't been Finn, she knew that. Noah, maybe? Maybe he was still alive. She trod lightly and sideways into the vegetation at her side, plotting a line around the back of Noah's position, one eye in the escarpment's direction, but the ever-darkening night hindered her view. The sight on her assault rifle took a helmet-mounted night vision link as the norm, but today was far from normal. It had been a day exercise, and she was the vehicle machine gunner. Each step took her nearer to confrontation, to conflict. This was a time to live or die.

Lisilo budi hutendwa. It has to be done.

But I want to live.

Zuri heard the crashing through the branches and bushes way before she saw the figure dashing towards her, lit by a yellow swirling light as it powered on. It appeared oblivious to her at first and she took the opportunity to fire a burst from the assault rifle. At thirty yards the bullets hammered against the plate, shattering on impact. The figure staggered slightly but pushed on through, the servos at its knees and hips whirring under the strain. Zuri let loose with another burst as the gap closed, knowing she'd hit home at such close range. Again, it took the hits though plates cracked and split. But this time the soldier went spinning out to her right and brought the yellow edged sword swinging down towards her shoulder. With the grace of a gymnast, Zuri pulled her shoulder back with her hip and leg swiftly following. Her stance was balanced as the enemy's body slammed into her, following through on the sword stroke. Zuri rode the hit, taking the blow to her right side but allowing her body to bend against the power as she spun back. Now facing the enemy's back, she put three rounds into his vertebrae plate at point blank range. The armour shattered; the black material rippled as it dissipated the kinetic impact. It held its integrity.

Stay down.

The servos whirred at hip, knee and elbow as the sword came streaking across her vision. A backwards left-handed blow swept round towards her waist. Training kicked in and intuitively Zuri raised her rifle to block the blow, again spinning left to reduce the impact. The sword sliced down into the barrel and on through towards the trigger grip. As Zuri's whirl reduced the momentum of the blow, she wrenched the rifle through the last of its arc and away from the blade with little to spare. Momentum carried her away from the enemy, they were briefly back-to-back.

Zuri ran, legs and heart pumping. Her mind raced with options, but she had only two. As she drove on, she took the path the enemy had taken, the clearest route and the one leading to Noah. Despite the blood rushing to her ears, she could hear the pursuit, but further back than she expected.

Maybe option two, then.

As Noah came in to sight, she could see he was bound. Awash with relief, her eyes desperately searched for his rifle as she sprinted forward. It lay in pieces nearby. Zuri picked a patch of ground and slid to a halt; dropping the rifle grip she swung round and held the other piece of the rifle in the direction she had come from. It was going to be close; Zuri flipped the safety and fired the grenade launcher.

Arm, you bloody grenade, arm.

At thirty-nine feet the grenade armed, at forty-one feet it smashed into the already fragile front armour of the enemy figure running towards her. At forty-two feet those plates gave out and shrapnel shredded the kinetic gel and the body behind. Zuri slammed into the forest floor as twisted metal flew her way. The bushes and trees around them both strummed with impacts.

Noah.

Chapter 35

As the sun finally dropped behind the hills, Smith heard renewed fighting to the southeast of the escarpment. The burst of SA80 gunfire pierced the forest to his left, quickly followed by others that were, in his experience, close to point-blank. The impacts echoed soon after.

Come on, take Three Scar down.

Then came the pop of the grenade launch, and as the sound of the explosive impact bounced off the escarpment wall Smith's two remaining captors moved. Clearly jittery, one eyed the forest with the double-barrelled rifle fixed on where the violence had reignited. The other jabbed at their tablet with increased anxiety. Their armour had faded to a deep blue-grey against the darkening woodland and their polarised visors had adjusted to a clear view. For the first time Smith could see their eyes and a moment of realisation swept through him, his denials in pieces as deep, black pupils gathered in the minimal light. Below each eye sat a spiral tattoo. Alien.

Smith was a man of training and discipline. The real world, where everything had its place. Those eyes did not belong. That doorway did not belong.

I do not belong.

Smith took a step back -the urge to run was strong. Duty held him in place, even in the face of the unknown. If he ran, he would still add further problems to whoever was out there. The tablet clipped to his side, the anxious alien lifted Smith to his feet, careful to keep him in the way of any potential gunfire. They moved together towards the metalled wall, the alien slipping its holstered weapon from a belt along the way. Roughly turned to face the doorway, Smith heard the scrape of a knife against the band binding his wrists. Blood rushed into his hands, and Smith flexed his fingers to relieve the numbness.

A now-familiar series of words and vocalised clicks filtered through the mask, punctuated with gestures towards the door. When Smith didn't move the alien grabbed his left hand, pressing it against the featureless door. A warmth spread through his palm. The surface layer of his skin moistened, soon followed by a series of deep needles piercing his palm and the radial artery in his wrist. That section of the wall pulsed with a blue light. Smith was too shocked to react, almost glued to the door in that instant. He was in the middle of a real-life sci-fi movie, and he hated that crap.

I repeat, this can't be happening. This is the really real world.

The needles withdrew, and Smith felt the skin on his palm detach. It didn't hurt, almost as if a surface layer had peeled away. As he removed his hand, the skin cells absorbed into the smooth wall before his eyes. Aghast, Smith looked at his reddening palm and back at the wall. There was a puncture hole just below his wrist, but no blood seeped out and he could see a hardened gel plugging the wound.

What? Have I been sampled?

The alien's gauntleted hand reached out and lightly stroked the spot where the skin had been absorbed. It still pulsed in a steady rhythm. The alien technician stepped back, taking out its tablet, gun still in hand. Awkwardly, it scanned the door whilst keeping him in sight.

Now?

Smith stole a glance at the alien watching the woods. The guard's enormous eyes were hugely dilated; its appearance gnawed at Smith's already frayed nerves. The menacing weapon moved in its hands, tracking something in the trees.

The technician at the door pressed sections in sequence, each lighting blue and pulsing with the rhythm of the first. On the eighth press a motor whirred, and a sense of dread washed over Smith as the opening door slowly exposed the void behind. Cold, ancient air washed over his face. The smell was sterile, like a morgue. Every hair on Smith's body stood on end.

And then the alien fired.

Chapter 36

The Escarpment, Garshellach Forest
15:46 GMT / 10:46 EST

Zuri ran the razor-edged knife through the ties at Noah's ankle and wrists. The material was plastic-like and split easily against the hardened blade. Noah's grateful nod belied the pain he felt along his upper right arm where the shrapnel had hit. Just a small piece had driven in where his combat armour ended. The muscle hadn't been torn but he'd need a tourniquet and medical assistance soon.

"Finn?" she mouthed to Noah, keeping their silence. Noah shrugged, raising his eyebrows at the same time. Zuri nodded and reloaded the battered grenade launcher with her penultimate round.

Finn, or check on the arsehole with the sword?

She couldn't risk the alien being alive at their rear, and who knew what the last two were up to. At least they hadn't joined in the fight, she stood little chance against three. Zuri moved off from freeing Noah; holding the grenade launcher in her right hand she signalled him to stay, knowing full well he wasn't fit enough to help right now. Zuri stooped low, hurrying as she saw the blade-wielding soldier laying still on the floor ahead. As she neared, there was a laboured chest movement as he fought for breath. A flutter from his thumb and forefinger confirmed her suspicions. She kicked the sword away; its edge had lost the luminescent shine. There was a deep hole in one side of the chest plate, punched through to the cavity within, blood mixed with the green gel oozing from beneath the ceramic plating.

The now transparent visor had cracked, and she could see straight to the wide-eyed woman within. One eye was clouded, the other full of hate. Clawed tattoos ran down both cheeks and up through the brow line. Zuri reached behind the mask and undid the clasp, lifting it away. A bubble of scarlet slipped from her thin lips. She had a pronounced and wide nose, similar to her compatriot's. There was a natural indentation in the skull, just above her right lobe, obvious but covered in fine hair. A gasping, wheezing set of clicks and garbled words emanated from her mouth, buzzing with anger. Zuri felt a familiarity with the sound, an emotional tug, a fragment of memory she could not grasp.

Looking away, Zuri placed a hand over the woman's mouth and eased her knife towards the exposed neck. In her mind she visualised digging the knife deep into her throat, the blade biting in where the windpipe should be. Snicking one of the carotid arteries on its journey through. The laboured breathing would come to an end, the anger draining from her good eye.

Adui wa mtu, ni mtu. The enemy of man is man.

But I am not my enemy.

As Zuri removed her hand away, she looked to the hate-filled eye of her foe. Recognition flickered in that eye; she knew Zuri had chosen to give life. The gauntleted hand slid the sidearm from the holster; it was halfway out before Zuri's knife bit home. Blood flowed as the pistol slipped to the forest floor. The laboured breathing stopped.

Zuri reached for the weapon at its grip, but as her hand neared a warning red glow pulsed from the strangely configured pistol. Zuri withdrew her fingers quickly. Looking over to the dulled sword, she came to the same conclusion.

Not for me.

She rasped the bloodied knife along the grass then slipped it back into its sheath. With the grenade launcher returned to her hands she headed on back, focussing on Noah. The shock of close combat would engulf her if she let it in; Finn had suffered for years as the distress of conflict battered at his mind. Finn needed her wherever she was. Fear of loss would incapacitate her just as much as the stress and trauma of taking a life, decisive actions impossible amongst hesitation and self-doubt. That way lay a darkness of spirit, and she had been there before. At thirteen, her world full of racism and hate, she had taken the first pill. But she had fought back.

We survive. Nobody harms me or mine without retribution.

Zuri reached Noah. He had taken a low ready position with his knife loose in his hands, eyes on the escarpment in the deepening murk of forest dusk. A rough tourniquet was on his upper arm, his first aid field kit buttoned back on his webbing belt. Zuri tapped him on the shoulder on the way past and urged him to follow. They stalked along the broken vegetated path left by the charging hostile. After just under a minute, they came across Finn's motionless body prostrate on the ground next to his smashed weapons. He was unbound and helmetless.

Zuri choked back her first thoughts, forcing the hot tears away. The thumping of her heart pounded against her chest, beating a rhythm of loss and anguish. She looked down at her tattooed hand, the semi-colon.

My time is not finished, my sentence not done. I survived and will survive.

Noah made to pass Zuri, pulling her back. Zuri sucked in a breath and gave Noah the full glare. She had stood down Lieutenant Bhakshi with that look, just the once, but he'd never forgotten or forgiven. And now he never would. Noah's resolve wilted under the full power of Zuri's will. This was for her to do. Noah lifted the strip of cloth in his hand and proffered it forward, indicating towards her eyes.

Maybe Finn's undervalued you, Noah. Maybe I have, too.

Zuri slipped her waterproof from her personal equipment, always useful in Scotland. Unzipped, she handed it to Noah and demonstrated what she wanted him to do. Noah nodded. She reached for a fist-sized rock to her left and a small stone. She needed to make a decision.

A fizzing shot from the escarpment quickly made up her mind. It was wild, but the powerful weapon smashed in to the thick branches above her head. Another shot thudded into the ground behind Noah, a third could take any of them out. Zuri dropped the stone and sprinted for Finn's prone body. Sliding to a halt just beside him, her back was towards the forest. She immediately sensed the drone rise from its hiding place; the movement of the air a giveaway. It would be low; this thing targeted the eyes.

Seeing his chance, Noah sprung forward, leaping with the waterproof ahead of him. As he came down, the coat enveloped the drone. The strobe fired, but Noah had already looked away and closed his eyes. He hoped it was enough. Resisting the pull of the coat, the drone urged itself upwards just as Zuri's rock came crashing down.

"No time," exclaimed Zuri. She prayed the rock strike was enough.

Another shot came crashing in, missing her by inches. It buried itself in the floor near Noah as he rolled backwards, wrapping the whirring drone in the coat as he went. Zuri lifted the grenade launcher, estimated the angle and fired. At this distance she didn't know whether it would have much impact; the tattooed leader had taken a real beating before his armour failed. As the grenade exploded, Noah smashed his wrapped package against a fir tree and left it there.

Zuri was already at Finn's body, the empty UGL at her side.

"Be alive, please be alive." Seeing no physical injury or wound, she placed her hand over his mouth and nose. The gentlest of breaths warmed her hand.

Zuri slapped his face hard, grabbed him by the forearms and pulled towards the far edge of the escarpment. Finn remained a dead weight, unmoving. But Zuri was strong, powerful and driven.

Chapter 37

Smith recognised the thump of the grenade launcher, instantly slamming into the alien technician in front of him as he leapt through the door. The explosion roared in his ears as the grenade hit its mark five feet above the alien guard. No shrapnel could reach them inside the door as Smith landed on the alien's armoured legs.

Now.

Smith scrabbled up the alien's back, reaching for the rifle strapped there. Servos heaved as the alien move to roll him off, but Smith's hands reached the grip way before then. The red warning glowed angrily as Smith took hold, heat surging through his hand. Self-preservation kicked in and he instinctively let go before any damage could be done. Smith pummelled at the back of the alien's helmet, smashing its head into the ground. The alien's knee and hip motors whirred, and Smith found himself thrown from the alien's back. Using the momentum, he continued the roll to come up on his feet. Between him and the alien lay the sidearm.

How good are you? Time to put that pressure on.

Smith feinted to the right, then went low on his left as the alien reacted. Smith's boot lashed at the gun, sending it spinning out the open door. Once more he continued the motion and came up facing the alien as it charged him, hands out, ready to grab. Smith rocked back, taking the arm and letting the alien's momentum carry it over his hip. He threw it against the wall.

Uki-goshi. Judo, Earth-style.

Smith locked the arm, pressing his boot under the alien's neck and helmet. Increasing the pressure slowly, he pushed in to where the creature's windpipe and carotid artery should be. The alien thrashed at Smith, hopelessly trying to find a way out of the choke hold, but Smith held all the aces. On its back, with its other arm unable to swing over, it was pinned. The servos in its locked elbow strained against Smith but he knew he had it.

But not the time to finish it. The guard likely survived that hit and there's no way I can crush a windpipe with all that armour. Does it even have one?

At that point, the alien stopped resisting. Its body seemed inert, however it was still breathing. Smith gave it twenty more seconds, though it felt like an age to him. He knew he had very little time once he released, maybe thirty seconds before it regained consciousness. Maybe a minute to be fully functional.

Smith released and headed inwards. After two strides the walls emitted a blue glow. Everything was a silver-blue metallic, including the second door another two steps in front of him. There was a panel beside it, pulsing with blue light.

Can it be that obvious? I hate this extra-terrestrial crap. I didn't even like ET.

Smith planted his hand on the panel, the door shifting in and to the side. Another waft of stale, sterile air assaulted his nose. With trepidation he stepped through–no time to waste.

Chapter 38

The Escarpment, Garshellach Forest
15:48 GMT / 10:48 EST

Noah knew that his body was stressed after the seizure. His brain not far behind in the anxiety stakes considering the last few hours. Yet somehow, up to now, he was coping. Since failing to join the RAF he had put himself through every extreme sport he could afford, short of flying in a wingsuit, which was next on his long list. He'd never been one for hitting the gym; still thin and gangly, he was often wrongly regarded as clumsy. But the sight of Zuri so desperate for Finn to live as she dragged him through the undergrowth was pushing his cortisol stress hormones to new levels.

"What now?"

"We move!" force-whispered Zuri. "Thermal imaging, night sights, whatever. We keep moving."

Noah looked down; there was Finn's helmet and the grenade launcher on the forest floor. Noah grabbed the UGL, he couldn't carry both and Finn with his injured arm. Noah caught up and took hold of Finn's legs. They both spun round and with Noah now in the lead they doubled their speed into the woods.

Just thirty more yards to the outcrop wall. But what then? Why aren't we heading deeper in the forest?

Twenty seconds later they reached the rock wall; no shots had been fired in the minute or so since Zuri had launched the last grenade, but it didn't feel over. Not at all. Zuri directed them behind a set of fallen rocks, setting up Finn in a sitting position.

"Keep down, Noah. The rocks need to be between you and them."

Noah looked round their new position. Zuri had chosen a spot where they were surrounded by the rock fall from the escarpment. Keep low enough and they'd be unseen by thermal and night vision systems.

And I thought I was the clever one.

Zuri had her canteen out, dripping water into Finn's mouth and splashing some on his hot cheeks.

"Slapping him won't bring him round," said Noah.

"I know, but it made me feel better. He scared the hell out of me." Zuri gave Noah a quick glance. "How come you recovered so quick?"

"If it's like my cousin's epileptic seizures, then everyone is different. Some fit for longer, others come out faster. Besides, I don't think I got a full hit off the strobe."

Zuri nodded at his response as a moan slipped from Finn's mouth. She turned to face him, watching his eyes flutter open.

"I have a big bastard of a headache," Finn stated, his red-rimmed eyes seeking out Zuri. "And my cheeks hurt like hell."

"Do you remember what happened?" Noah asked, checking on Finn's state of confusion.

"Yep, drone plus stupid squaddie equals lights out."

Finn massaged the back of his neck, circling his shoulders to ease out the aches he had there. "Sit rep?"

"Zuri took out one hostile and had run-ins with the drones. We've been shot at as we rescued you, probably from the target site. Zuri responded with a grenade and we've heard nothing for a few minutes. It's likely we have two hostiles and Smith out there. We are about fifty yards from the target. Zuri has assumed they have thermal and night vision capability so here we are amongst the rocks." Finn nodded, then winced as Noah finished his report.

"Weapons?"

"One grenade launcher and one grenade. Oh, and three knives. Assuming you have your knife, that is," interjected Zuri.

"That it?"

Zuri nodded. "Yep."

"Then it's impossible. Even without potential thermal and night vision we don't stand a chance against their level of capability. We try, we die." Finn hated saying it.

"What about rescue? It's been over an hour since first contact, about fifty minutes in pursuit. They could be close." Zuri willed it to be true. "We can sit and wait, report and support. We can still be some use to Smith."

"If, and I mean if, they didn't track us to this position then it's a good option. Noah?" Noah twitched, not expecting to be asked his opinion.

"I'm in. Finish the job. Save Smith."

Stop babbling.

"OK, here's the dilemma. We step out to see if we are being tracked, we get seen. We don't check, we are sitting ducks."

Zuri sighed.

Chapter 39

Smith stood just a step inside the room. The stone walls were covered in stunningly colourful batiks, the floor in luxurious rugs woven from hair and interspersed with huge, fleeced animal skins. Arranged around these were comfortable-looking cushions in apparently scattered piles across the room. In the corner a strange contraption, a hybrid mix of strings and percussion, possibly a sculpture or an instrument that stretched up towards the vaulted ceiling. Maybe both.

Smith spied the next opening, doorless and leading on to another room behind. In the low light that reached it he could just make out desks shaped from the volcanic rock served by wooden chairs. All the proportions seemed out of kilter, familiar items yet odd to the eye.

Good to know there's something normal after all the crazy sci-fi stuff.

Glancing to his left, Smith's hopes resurfaced. A rack of four weapons the likes of which he'd never seen before hung on the wall. The first, a strange combination of spear and rifle, shimmered under the ceiling's glow. It was easily four feet long with a defined grip and trigger positioned one third of its length from the base. The seamless ivory stock shaped to fit a shoulder larger than his, and his fingers would struggle to reach the trigger, but he'd manage. Attached to the bottom of the rifle's barrel a long metal rod extended beyond its muzzle and ended with a razor-sharp spear head.

Now that's what I'm talking about.

Smith grabbed the weapon, ignoring the assembly of strange armaments at its side and not sparing a glance for the one empty space. There simply wasn't time, the alien would surely be coming round by now and he'd seen nothing of the other guard.

Smith adjusted his right hand on the grip, feeling the incredibly light weight and balance. But somehow it felt inert, unready for combat. Dead. He searched the weapon frantically for an 'on' button. There was no space for a magazine, nor any evidence of a breech loading system for a single bullet. When he turned the weapon over, he found a recess in the fore-end of the gun, just where his left thumb should sit. The base of the square edged hole was metallic. Something had to fit in there.

Smith scanned the rack, his survival instincts screaming at the lack of time he had left. Three gauntleted fingers gripped the edge of the doorway; his nemesis pulled itself through still groggy but with clear intent. Its sidearm, threatening and menacing, sat in its right hand. As the creature brought the gun round Smith struck with the spear, bayonet style, between the upper and lower torso plates. The sharpened point split the armour's black material, the kinetic gel spilling out. Smith lunged harder, feeling the spear scrape against an inner layer of ceramics and pushing his adversary off balance. His forefinger stretched for the trigger, pulling it in desperation. But nothing happened.

Damn.

Smith leaned back, tugging the bladed weapon out as the unbalanced alien tried to bring its weapon to bear. Smith brought it down on the alien's outstretched arm, the hardened spear edges smashing the servos at the elbow joint. The sidearm hit the floor, and Smith kicked it away.

I won't survive fighting the old way. That armour is straight out of a bloody computer game.

Rather than charging in, Smith jumped back towards the rack, eyes on the alien as it scrambled to regain its feet.

Come on. Something, give me something.

As Smith scanned across the weapons rack, he caught sight of a recess above the empty space. It exactly matched the one on his weapon. His brain compensated for the light with that knowledge, and he noted a square outline

99

directly above each one.

This sci-fi weirdness is going to be the death of me.

Smith pressed his left hand in to the square above the riflespear's space. On contact, Smith felt his mind being sucked out through his fingers. Squeezed and stretched through the tiniest space, it thrummed and expanded as it swept into the small metallic square. And then it really went weird.

Smith spun along a highway of lights, each ranged out ahead in a maelstrom of swirls and tangents. Initially, he raced along one radiant lane only for it to split in to two, three, four ways. His body sliced into sections as if ready for a microscope and separated to follow each one. Split and split again, each splice thinner and thinner. Disconnected. Each cell in his body stripped down to its base components. Amongst this turmoil the sense of examination pervaded, as if his very spirit was a mere subject of scientific curiosity. The sense of loss was absolute.

Ahead, the lights unified. His spliced and sectioned body precisely slotted together as each illuminated tangent merged in to the next. He was Smith again, but Smith as he was born, as he grew, as he loved, as he cried. Memories flooded through him from birth to childhood, from childhood to manhood. His first kiss, his first kill, all laid bare for all to see.

Smith's mind slammed back into his body. Time had stood still, his finger still upon the metal square that popped up from the wall. Without thinking he grabbed it and slotted it in place. The weapon came alive in his hands, he could feel a surge run along its entire length. Pulses of effervescent light flowed along the barrel.

Game over.

A cheek caressed a familiar stock. Eyes tracked through a long-used sight. A finger pulled a well-known trigger. The smell of his favourite gun oil drifted up his nose. A thousand times he had stripped it down and rebuilt it, his best friend. As Smith shot, a three-round burst flew from his beloved SA80 A2 assault rifle drilling home at point blank range into the alien's lower chest plates. The ceramic shattered, and the bullets reached the flesh behind. A second burst was unnecessary, but after the day he'd had Smith really wanted to make sure.

If he respawns, I'm out of here.

Smith blinked, looking down at the weapon in his hands. It was his gun, down to the nicks and scratches it had suffered over the years. The only difference was in the fore-end, a small metal slab sat there, just where his thumb would be. Smith raised his eyebrows as he gave the gun a once-over. Nothing was ever going to surprise him again after today.

My weapon of choice.

Chapter 40

The Escarpment, Garshellach Forest
15:51 GMT / 10:51 EST

"Well?" asked Corporal Lumu.

"I get heat signatures from the western end of the rock face. Muddled, but definitely two figures there, possibly three. On night vision there's a hint of a standard infantry helmet. Can't be sure, but I'm betting this is our squad." Mills' voice filtered through the radio.

Lumu flicked down his own goggles attached to his helmet; night vision only, but good enough. He sighted down the SA80 A3.

"There's still only one hostile in that doorway. Looks like they've had a firefight of some form. There's an impact zone to the right of him, possibly a grenade. Doesn't seem that injured but heavily distracted. He should have eyes on us if he's using thermal, but I have no sign he is."

"Corporal, I have eyes on and have the shot," McCloud whispered through the PRR. The troop's sharpshooter never overstated. If he had the shot, he had the shot. But they'd all seen that armour and they weren't packing the sniper rifle McCloud favoured. Would it have punched through any weak spots? Possibly, but without examining a set who knew.

"Negative, McCloud." Too professional to complain, but Lumu knew he'd be moaning silently in a broad Scottish accent.

"You have incoming, I repeat, y —... have incoming." Lumu's channel to the helicopter crackled and faded in and out. He'd left it open for relayed orders from command, but they were at the extreme end of their range. "Four aircraft heading your way, same..." Lumu's eyes flickered to the tree canopy. "Typh—… in purs—…"

Decision time. We'll be outgunned if they land. If we could catch them as they do, we may have a chance.

Two Typhoons roared over the tree canopy, swiftly followed by the sound of their Mauser cannons firing off in bursts. Corporal Lumu decided there and then. If the Typhoons were reduced to cannons, it meant they were out of air-to-air missiles or the radar guidance wasn't effective. Gunfire punctuated his thoughts, echoing from the doorway.

"McCloud, Thompson, target the guard at the door on my mark. Mills, track the figures you've picked up. Any hint they are hostiles I want a sit rep immediately. We may be about to have company at the rear, so stay frosty and alert."

Corporal Lumu of the Elite SAS reserve peered down his sight, night vision goggles giving him a clear view. "Mark."

Chapter 41

The Escarpment, Garshellach Forest
15:51 GMT / 10:51 EST

Sweat poured off Finn's head as the after-effects of the drone-induced seizure continued to bother him. He swept his hand over his sodden scalp. He couldn't decide if he was in a terrible mood or just a bad one. They'd come out of the combat situation in one piece–well, mostly. Noah had a piece of shrapnel stuck in him and his headache was a doozy. Zuri was battered and bruised.

But she's alive and that's all that counts.

"Finn," whispered Noah, "Two Typhoons incoming, Mark 4 with that rumble." Finn's ears attuned to a low vibration that quickly escalated to the roar of low flying jets. They all ducked down as the cannon fire sounded off.

"How the hell…" shouted Zuri. Noah just raised his eyebrows in response.

Immediately, the sound of gunfire followed. Finn knew that sound: multiple SA80s, possibly A3s but aimed at the escarpment, not at them. Finn scrambled to his feet, followed by Zuri and Noah. Reaching down for his helmet, he realised he had none. There was a call from the woods to their right, one he knew well, in the gloom he made out a figure issuing the signal for 'friend', then a 'follow me'.

Quickly, Zuri took point, the last grenade loaded. Noah was behind with Finn at the rear, feeling naked without his helmet. They relied on the eyes of the lead soldier heading straight towards the centre of the escarpment as the clatter of more assault rifle fire echoed through the evening. There was a single boom of return fire, followed by a tree exploding to their left.

The intensity of the assault rifle fire increased, but something was wrong. One set was now aimed away from the fight, and the bursts slewed into continuous fire. It wasn't going well over there, someone was under heavy, life-threatening stress. They reached a rockfall, thirty feet from a doorway that Finn knew hadn't been there before.

Got to trust this soldier knows what he's doing.

Chapter 42

Inside the Escarpment, Garshellach Forest
15:51 GMT / 10:51 EST

The clatter of assault rifle fire knocked Smith out of his revelry. He quickly checked the room, eyes scrutinising the open doorway for any danger. Dismissing the risk, Smith moved to the edge of the main doorway. He needed to see round but he had little choice other than to charge on through. The sense that someone was waiting for him to do that was very strong, but he'd trained for this.

Admittedly, a grenade would be a safer bet.

Smith calmed his breathing and went through low, assessing the room ahead in an instant. The guard squatted at the corner of the main door, bullets ricocheting against the metal door and the walls beyond. Its armour displayed multiple hits; some plates were cracked though most appeared functional. However, its helmet leaked gel and the ceramic plating around its neck was in a mess. He was firing outwards, towards the woods.

Smith didn't hesitate, firing two bursts into the alien's upper back followed by one to the head. It went down, blood pumping and pitching forwards through the threshold. Not his favourite thing to do, yet their firepower and armour meant he simply couldn't take the risk. The damage to the head confirmed the kill, but he took no pleasure from it.

Smith moved cautiously over to the left side of the door, away from the alien corpse. The flash of gunfire flared dead ahead. He recognised the pattern, buddy team covered withdrawal. These were friendly soldiers fending off an attack now. He raised his rifle to use the SUSAT optical sight as best he could, wishing for a full ARILLS thermal night sight he had tried out for a few weeks last year.

The specs on that thing were amazing.

Smith removed his eye and blinked out the sweat and grit. As he looked back through the sight, a clear thermal image appeared. Two experienced soldiers were moving back in unison, taking position to cover the other in turn. As he scanned outwards, Smith caught the far less obvious image of three advancing figures, shots appearing as tracer bullets in the gathering darkness. Their movements were highly professional, too.

Keep this up and I'll be knocking my heels together and wishing for a Challenger Mark 2 tank.

Smith fired, single shots targeting the advancing figures, trying to delay them by forcing them to cover. He swiftly switched between targets, continuing to slow their advance though none stayed permanently down under his hail of bullets.

I wonder what happens when the magazine is empty?

Smith took aim again, noting a brief flicker of warmth in his cross hairs just to the right of his intended target. As he adjusted his aim, a tracer trail streaked along his eyeline, coming straight for him.

The explosion reverberated around the room, echoing out through the forest. But Smith didn't hear any of it, his torn and broken body awkwardly angled against the wall. His *weapon of choice* lay by his side, his left hand upon the stock, his thumb upon the plate.

Chapter 43

Doorway, The Escarpment, Garshellach Forest
15:52 GMT / 10:52 EST

As the dust flew and the roar of the explosion washed over the tree, Finn hit the dirt. Ahead, the leading soldier had taken the backwash from the detonation across his combat armour. He was down, struggling for breath. Zuri grabbed the straps of his kit and dragged him the last few feet towards the edge of the door. Finn caught up, keeping low, and followed suit. Noah picked up his dropped weapon and spun to face the forest as two more soldiers backed in to view. Noah blindly fired into the trees, hoping to give cover.

As they hit the doorway, Finn took stock of the room. Smith lay in a tangled mess on one side of the room. Blood pooled underneath him, but Finn knew his heart wasn't pumping. Shattered bones poked out from his combat fatigues. Dead.

Damn.

Two incoming rounds hit the side of the wall. As they smacked into the metal, Finn ducked down, mindful of the ricochet. When he looked back up the rounds were drilling wildly into the wall, a whirr of fury and heat. It was the ammunition they used to take down the Bulldog.

"Finn, here," called Zuri over the din of the angry rounds.

She reached down and grabbed Smith's helmet from his left hand and threw it over. No choice in the heat of battle; Finn slid it over his head, the strap under his chin.

"Sorry, Smith."

"That's okay," came the reply over the radio.

Zuri took up position on the left of the main door, "Grenade heading south, move," her last grenade already leaving the UGL as she shouted. Noah pelted through the doorway, swiftly followed by an SAS corporal who span and sent a burst back through as the *whomp* of the grenade made its mark.

"Finn, through the next door. Move, Lance Corporal."

"Next room," bellowed Finn. Grabbing the stricken soldier, he urgently pulled towards the beckoning doorway. "Please, Zuri, move." Zuri, headstrong to the last, followed. All hope of any other survivors lost, her heart weighed heavy as she followed Finn through the door.

"Hit the button on your right. Do it, soldier!"

Finn slammed his palm against the glowing raised square in the wall, following orders. Zuri supported their wounded colleague as Finn passed him over, moving out of the line of fire. Corporal Lumu and Noah followed, taking high and low position guard either side of the second door, both trying to slow their breathing after the firefight.

The main door silently slid out on top and bottom hinges and flowed in to place. It sealed itself shut with a gentle hiss as the sound of gunfire clattered against it.

Zuri blew a huge sigh as she gently let the wounded man slip to the floor. The uniform shouted SAS and having seen the effectiveness of the retreat, she didn't doubt her judgement. "Corporal, you want to check on your wounded man?"

"Could you do so, Lance Corporal. I trust your actions will be as good as mine," stated Corporal Lumu. "I'm Lumu, SAS reserve, by the way. And that's Trooper Mills." Lumu's eyes never wavered off the door.

"Lance Corporal Zuberi. Scots Reserve trainer." Zuri bent to tend to Mills, feeling for the cracked ribs she fully expected to find. The wince told her all she needed to know.

"Hopefully soon-to-be Private Stephen Noah, the trainee."

Finn, back to the wall, slid down to a sitting position. His breath felt heavy, the headache thrumming at his nerves as he pressed two fingers into the bridge of his nose.

"Lance Corporal Finn, Scots Reserve trainer," stated Finn with some bitterness.

"Corporal Smith, Squad Leader Scots Reserves training section," spoke Finn's personal radio into his ear.

Finn sat up straight, startled. Realisation hit home about the orders he'd followed. His eyes searched the room frantically for any sign of Smith. But he knew where he was, he'd seen the smashed body.

"Now, I don't want you to panic, Finn. If you'd had my day, this would seem pretty normal."

The sudden strangled cry from Finn startled Zuri as he frantically tore Smith's helmet off, throwing it across the room. She looked up from her ministrations, taking the throw as a show of stress and anger. The loss of Smith may have triggered his last step in to the depths of PTSD. She couldn't blame him; he'd kept it together so far but there was only so much any of them could take. One look at Finn's screwed-up face seemed to confirm her worries. She eased Mills into a set of cushions, slipping a single-use ice pack from her first aid kit under his armour.

Zuri moved to kneel by Finn, not giving a thought for protocol. She reached out and stroked the hair above his ear and down the back of his neck. Her eyes slid over his, looking for the signs that he was slipping away. There was a tremble to him, but it had been there since the drone attack, maybe even after he'd found Kapoor and Cillian. She allowed him to slip into the crook of her arm. Stuff protocol, Lumu could report her to whoever he liked.

Jicho la moyo linaona mengi. The heart's eye sees many things, my dear Finn.

"I think I may be going mad," whispered Finn. Zuri looked down at him, a worried frown appeared.

"After all we've been through, I think we may all be a little screwed up, Finn," Zuri spoke with a softness that defied her worries.

"I'm hearing things, Zuri. How did I know to close the door, Zuri? How?" Finn replied.

"That was me," came a voice very much like Smith's, the helmet radio's volume way beyond its usual maximum.

Zuri and Noah looked from Finn to the helmet and back. Shock reflected in their faces at what they'd just heard. It sounded like Smith; the tone was certainly his drawl. Corporal Lumu glanced behind him for the first time, wary of what was in front but concerned about what was happening behind.

"My PRR shutdown when we entered this building. I have no outside contact. How come you are receiving, Lance Corporal Finn?"

"I'm not, mine was burnt out during the attack on Field Command. That's Smith's helmet. Or one he picked up on the way here."

"Smith?"

"The dead Corporal smashed against the wall in that room." Finn pointed angrily, desperately not wanting to think about it. "He's the one we came to rescue."

Corporal Lumu peered into the room in front, taking in the corporal stripes and the bloody mess of the body. He signalled for Noah to stay put with eyes on the main door, walking over to the discarded helmet. Pulling off his own, he swapped helmets over so he could use the microphone comfortably. As he did so, Zuri noted the metal plate stuck to the back. It had a lustre similar to the metalled walls the door was set in. Throughout, Lumu pointedly kept his eyes averted from Finn and Zuri.

That's not standard issue.

"This is D Air Troop Number 1, Corporal Lumu calling. Please respond." It was clear Lumu was receiving an instant response, though the volume had thankfully been toned down. As he listened, his gaze switched between the rag tag soldiers within the room. He listened intently, nodding.

Finn had sat up, watching the SAS man with intense interest. Whatever was happening, at least the others could hear the voice. Maybe he was just shaken up about Smith's death; the violence and loss had been sudden and shocking. Smith had been their focus over the last hour or so, duty to their squad mate overriding their fear. But now they had failed. Finn's eyes took Zuri in ever so briefly: the curve of her mouth, the eyes that shone with a passion for life.

I can't let myself slip into the darkness. I can hold on.

"Okay," started Lumu, his back straight, but his face told a much more perplexed story than his body language allowed. He slipped off the helmet, turning it so the metal plate was visible to everyone. "That wasn't UK Special Forces command. It, or he, whatever, confirmed that Corporal Smith is in fact dead. The voice we can hear is a computer simulation recorded before his demise," Lumu tapped the plate for emphasis. "The computer insists that the aliens remain outside, but they have the capability to break in. Smith has witnessed this, the computer recorded it. It states categorically that our only hope is to gain control of the sensors and cameras linked to this building." Lumu coughed, clearly uncomfortable with his situation.

"How do we do that?" chipped in Noah. "By the looks of where we are, I'm guessing this isn't a standard army HQ."

"Plug me in to the main console in the next room," floated a sterile version of Smith's voice from the PRR, volume upped again. "I'm a recording of a human, perhaps I can adapt the interface to your needs."

"This day simply can't get any weirder," sighed Zuri, the cuts on her shoulder and neck standing out in the room's glow. "We are outmatched and if they get in, there's no surviving this day. I know we all want to live so what have we got to lose? Finn? Noah?"

"Since when has this been a democracy? Corporal Lumu, you are in charge," said Finn, desperate to pass on any responsibility to relieve the pressure of the darkness buzzing at edge of his mind.

Lumu stood next to the pile of giant cushions, his boots sole deep in an animal skin he didn't even recognise, with aliens pounding at the door. To top all that, there was a computer claiming to be a dead soldier. No comms, no orders and right now, no back up.

This is not a good day.

"What weapons and ammunition do we have?" He looked at each of them.

The count came back with two assault rifles and eighty rounds of ammunition, two Glock sidearms, around fifty rounds. No grenades. Grim.

"Do it." He threw the helmet to Finn. "It said this helmet belongs to you now and a soldier should never be without it." Finn stared at the thing nestling in his hands as Lumu moved to check on Mills for the first time.

Why me?

Finn looked in desperation towards Zuri, but Noah caught his eye.

"I can help, Corporal Finn. I'm better with computers than a gun."

Finn gave a relieved nod of approval. Noah offered Mills' assault rifle to Zuri, who was glad to have the reassurance of it in her hands. The safety was on, too. As Lumu checked on Mills' ribs, he admired the efficiency with which she switched magazines and took a ready position by the door. It nearly improved his mood. Nearly.

Finn and Noah moved through to the next room; the ceiling lit up with the strange light as they entered. The walls were covered in wafer-thin, curved screens that protruded from the walls. All were dark, lifeless. At the oddly angled stone table sat a set of three wooden chairs, each slightly out of proportion to the human norm. All the pieces of the room together made them both feel slightly uncomfortable, ill at ease with their surroundings. On the slabbed table in front of the middle chair sat a flat silver panel with a series of recesses of different sizes and depths. At the side were tumbled stacks of blue metal tablets made of the same material as the square on Finn's dreaded helmet.

Noah pulled out the middle chair and offered the spot to Finn, who flatly refused the offer. Noah sat down and carefully slipped Smith's plaque off the helmet and on to the table. Picking it up and selecting a slot of the same size he pushed it down in to place. A satisfying clunk resounded through the metal plaque.

Finn stood back, expecting a series of blinking lights and whirring noises as screens and keyboards appeared from nowhere. Instead, a three-foot high 3D holographic image of Smith appeared above the table. It flickered in and out, with Smith's image stretching and expanding in every direction before returning to normal proportions. He was wearing his parade uniform, it looked immaculate. His face was carefully shaven, hair trimmed to perfection. Finn was sure the look on his face was the one he saved especially for him, utter disappointment.

I don't like the look of this.

"Now I know I didn't handle this in the best way, Lance Corporal Finn. I've never been a computer programme before," stated the apparently apologetic holographic Smith. "But we need to pull together and save these soldiers. Duty and discipline can get us through if we have a plan."

It's Smith: the face, the mannerisms. The uniform.

"It looks like Corporal Smith to me, Lance Corporal," Noah's tone was reassuring, "and sounds like him."

The room's screens all switched on, the images were all 2D and in heavily blue tinged colour.

"I have–what's the phrase? Yes, I have 'shaken hands' with the House Artificial Intelligence and come to an accord, though it's wary of my human persona. It is however in agreement that the building has been attacked. It cannot override the door locking mechanism." The voice remained Smith's but without the emotion. Finn felt this Smith was really trying to keep him calm. Reduce the weirdness just a little.

"Corporal Lumu, we have visual," bellowed Finn.

Lumu hurried through, worried by leaving only Zuri near the door and an injured colleague between him and the enemy. But needs must.

All three scanned the screens showing a full surrounding view of the escarpment. Unnerving images showed two aliens stood guard at the door with a full view of the woods ahead. The others were clearly scanning the main door with tablet-like machines.

"The visuals are a compendium of enhanced images from what we would call night vision, thermal and other light-based wave lengths. It's in real time." Smith paused, thinking. "I would say, judging by my previous experience, we have around two minutes before they work out the combination of presses. The House agrees."

"What weapon systems does this facility have?" asked Lumu.

"None. At least none we can action from here. There are some portable weapons." Smith's 3D image visibly grimaced. "But they'll take some time to come up to full power once activated. From the little information I have from the AI we could arrange a distraction; they would leave and you can start getting the new weapons ready. But I don't know the consequences of that action."

Finn did not like the sound of that. "Consequences, Smith? Explain."

"The House AI won't let me access any of the data banks and it's avoiding my questions. But at the moment, I believe they are mistaken in targeting this facility. The House says they are seeking a ship. A spaceship." Smith appeared to pause again, deep in thought. "We have ninety seconds. The House can activate a signal beacon on that ship."

"Smith, set the distraction. We need the time for a full sit rep. All the information you can," ordered Lumu.

"Done." Smith faded away slightly, the image once again expanding and contracting. "Assimilating information, Corporal Lumu." They watched the screens for a reaction from the aliens at the door. Within a few seconds the two scanning came together, clearly having a conversation. Signals flew back and forth before they turned in unison and sent one guard out to the trees. A few seconds later, they returned with a body.

"That's McCloud. They took him out early on. He was on a small boulder, eyes on the original aliens." Lumu looked visibly distressed as he spoke, though as a Gurkha and SAS he suppressed it. Finn knew that feeling well, wanting to reassure the man but aware it wasn't the right thing to do now.

Grieve later, act now.

"What are they doing?" Lumu peered at the screen. The alien technicians had taken out a set of scalpels and swabs. With speed and efficiency, they worked around McCloud's body.

"Taking a sample of blood and DNA. And not in small quantities," said Smith. "The House AI says they plan to use it to gain entry to the spaceship. They believe the ship is keyed to our human DNA to enable access."

"Is that true?"

Smith's hologram visibly shrugged. "It won't say. It's like pulling teeth. It doesn't want to share anything that might compromise the owners of this House or the ship."

As Smith finished explaining the scalpels and swabs were slotted back into two bags along with a set of capsules. Each technician took one set of each. With a brief signal they brought out a small device and depressed one section of it. Immediately there was a brief flicker across each of the screens though Smith's hologram didn't alter. Reforming into buddy teams with the technicians split between them, they moved out.

"Was that an EMP?" asked Corporal Lumu to no one in particular.

Finn nodded. "Likely. The effects at Field Command and the area were extensive. Blew the radar systems and the radios. Thought all that was protected."

"It is, and it isn't," said Smith, "the House tells me that the sensors and cameras are still working because they have multiple fail-safes and multi-wavelength EMP shielding. However, that is an EMP emitter, not a simple grenade. It's sending repeated pulses. Your electronics will shield against one wavelength but not all, or shutdown and reset after each one. The results are the same, whilst in the vicinity shielded electronics will eventually short circuit, or your system keeps shutting down after each pulse rendering it inoperative. And before you ask, no, I have no idea of range or timescale. Bet they'll hide it in this locality."

"So, depending on the range, we are on our own for now," stated Lumu.

"But safe and alive," responded Zuri from the other room. "Under a rock in a steel box. We've just been through hell, Corporal. We are strung out, and have a rookie and an injured man amongst us."

"I am well aware of that. But we don't know the real consequences of releasing that ship to them. They want that ship for some powerful reason. They've taken significant risks against an army to do so without recourse to dialogue or negotiation. From what I understand there's been involvement at the top of UK Special Forces command and beyond." Lumu could see Zuri bristling. Finn glanced across at Lumu, managing a smirk despite the circumstances.

You haven't seen anything yet, Corp. Here it comes.

"With respect, Corporal, if you are saying we should go out there with limited weaponry and half a squad to recover a bunch of space technology we don't even know is there then you can stick your SAS insignia up y—" Zuri had taken a step through the door, guard duty lost amongst her roiling emotions. Was it anger, hope, despair or need? Did she even know?

"Zuri!" Finn stepped between Lumu and the advancing Zuri. Zuri's hands were flexing against the assault rifle. "Lance Corporal Zuberi of the Scots

Reserve," Finn enunciated each word slow and firm, "stand down."

Zuri threw Corporal Lumu a look of fury, and sparing little she gave Finn a similar glare as she spun and walked out the room. The atmosphere crackled as she left.

Lumu continued, unheeding of the warning Zuri had brought, "As I was saying, if they gain technology that is a danger to the citizens of the UK, even the rest of the world, we must act. We can't signal for help and we have no idea if anyone is coming soon. The area is now an EMP hotbed, so no helicopters can fly in nor can reconnaissance jets get close."

Finn knew where this was going, and although he didn't want to face any more combat, the argument was powerful. He felt the anxiety surge from the pit of his stomach.

Breathe.

"You mean we shouldn't have used the decoy?" said Noah.

"It bought us our lives and time to think," replied Lumu, his hand scraping along his jawline. "It was the right thing to do."

"Oh, crap," came from the holographic Smith. "I repeat, oh, crap. I have broken into a few data banks about the spaceship. The House said they were looking for 'a' ship. To be specific, what the AI calls a 'SeedShip', similar to one left on their planet by the same–" Smith's 3D image actually coughed, "–alien species that inhabited this House. I don't have the processing access or speed yet to analyse the information, but as far as I can gather our decoy ship is far more capable than this 'SeedShip' they are seeking." Smith appeared to look directly at Lumu. Finn knew exactly what the real Smith would say right now. "You are correct in your assessment, Corporal Lumu. It is our duty to act."

Knew it.

Chapter 44

Wildcat 1, Field Command
16:05 GMT / 11:05 EST

"Estimated arrival of the Apache is around an hour, Jenks. They ordered us to land at the aircraft crash site and allow Marshall to take our station up here. We need to conserve fuel." Ibrahim was worried; they had lost all contact with the SAS air troop some time ago, but orders were to hold.

Jenks nodded; his lip chewing had receded as the combat situation had calmed down. Even so, Ibrahim knew his sense of duty was still gnawing at him. He was worried about Finn and the rest of his squad having frequently worked together over the last two years. It was hard enough feeling the deaths of colleagues, worse if their friendship had been part of your life too.

Jenks suddenly jerked forward, wrestling with both pitch controls. The panel lights blinked out. The EMP warning light had been triggered, the rotor turbine whined. Flying Officer Ibrahim did not panic. They had trained for this. They knew their stuff. The helicopter shielding would adapt, the electronics would kick back in as the pulse passed. At his last check, their altitude would give them time for a restart of all systems.

Joy surged through Ibrahim as the panel lit and the whine of the rotors spun up. Jenks reacted with reflexes borne from hours of simulation and training. Within seconds he had the chopper back under control, breathing hard. His lip started bleeding.

"Well done, J —" then the next pulse hit and the Wildcat Mark 1 plummeted into the tree canopy.

Chapter 45

Inside the Escarpment, Garshellach Forest
16:06 GMT / 11:06 EST

Zuri seethed; Finn could see the tension in her body. He needed to be extremely wary of how he handled what was to come. He stood next to the arms rack Smith had directed him to, near to the door Zuri was guarding. She had heard every word from Lumu and Smith and was trembling.

Not the time to say I agree then.

No one had noticed the rack when they first raced into the room, being rather distracted by the need for safety. Next to the rack lay one alien–Smith called it a 'technician'–the tattoos were circular. Puncture marks at the edge of the left chest plate reflected what Smith had told them about the 'weapon' he had used. The bullet pattern from the SA80, though, was another story. Finn knew Zuri had laid point blank bursts into her assailant to no avail. These had ripped through.

"I warn you now," Smith's hologram took a breath, squeezing the point between his eyes where his nose should be, "take one of those metal plates and you'll be copied warts and all. It's some trip but it means the weapon can reach its full power, though the House says this takes time as the persona must be fully analysed before a proper connection is made."

There was no doubt they needed more firepower. He could see Zuri had turned from her post, a simmering stare giving him no quarter to avoid what was coming.

"So we're going, huh?" said Zuri.

"I am. You are getting Mills out of here. Taking Noah, too," said Finn, turning to face her.

"Who gets to decide that? You? We are the same rank, Lance Corporal Finn, lest you forget." Finn could feel the heat of her anger.

Decisions, decisions.

He reached out, again breaking the taboo of fraternisation. Gently, he touched her cheek with the back of his hand. Zuri knocked it away, eyes to the floor and boring a hole to the centre of the earth. Despondent, she eventually gave in, slowly reaching out and taking the same hand to place it back against her cheek.

"I need to survive, Finn. We need to survive. We have only just…" Finn moved his hands to her lips, unable to take what was coming if he was to face what lay ahead.

Found each other. We have only just found each other.

"I cannot be alone." Zuri reached up and touched the square slotted in the wall above the second weapon.

Umoja ni nguvu, utengano ni udhaifu. Strength together, being apart is weakness.

The light in Zuri's eyes briefly flickered and went out, almost imperceptible unless you were already gazing into them. Finn's chest ached, the heat of the flame and the smell of burnt flesh that haunted him in his lowest moments rose in his mind. But then she was back and, as always, her presence beat the demons away.

The square had lifted from its recess and dropped in Zuri's palm. Without looking at Finn she slipped the long, flat, triple-bladed sword from the weapons rack. The leather grip ended with a metal pummel, the hilt spiked upwards. It was the most unwieldy weapon Finn had ever seen. Zuri slotted the small plaque into the hilt of the blade, her thumb resting upon it as she gripped the sword. Zuri felt the weight. The balance was perfect for her as she moved it through the air.

I don't have a clue how to use a normal sword, never mind this monstrosity.

The image in Zuri's mind was of her real prowess, and she felt the handle morph and squirm briefly in her grip. The SA80 A3, the ARILLS sight and UGL grenade launcher now in her hand matched that image perfectly. If she hadn't seen it and felt it, she wouldn't have believed it had happened. She checked the grenade launcher's breech: loaded.

But I have only one.

"What a weird day," understated Finn. "I take it you're coming, then." At the back of his mind, he wondered what happened to the copies if they died. A question for another, more normal day perhaps. He picked up Zuri's discarded assault rifle, which she'd set aside for her shiny new one. Briefly glancing at Lumu, he handed it over to Noah.

"You're seeing Mills out, Private." Passing the weapon over to Noah, he gave him the full reassurance of a tap to his good arm. "You'll do fine."

"No, he's not." Lumu had been kneeling next to Mills in conversation. "Mills has a few broken ribs, but he can walk. We need as many soldiers as we can. Mills has the coordinates and knows the path back. He'll keep his radio off; as soon as he finds the range of the EMP, he can signal for help. With us, Noah, if you please."

"But..."

"With us, Private." Lumu stared at the weapons rack like it was a nest of serpents. "And take that weapon, if you please."

"You should..." started Noah, well aware of his position in the room.

"I cannot, Private. I will not. I wish to be reincarnated until my soul is liberated. I do not know, nor wish to know if that is possible if I am recorded upon that scrap of metal. That is my choice." Lumu set his jaw, clearly not taking questions about this choice, nor protests.

Noah stole a glance at Finn. He was clearly not happy with the decision. Was it Lumu not taking a weapon, or Noah being part of the squad?

I need to prove my worth. I need to choose wisely, but the possibilities I think are way beyond their choices.

Noah stepped forward, his decision already set in his mind. This was unlikely to be a close-quarter firefight, so could he be effective from a distance? He wasn't the best shot, but if he were to use something high powered, he didn't have to be that good!

Besides, from Smith's description, I think there's a little extra help available.

Noah placed his hand on the square above the next weapon; of all the weapons on the rack it was by far the simplest. If he didn't know any better, he would have described it as a stone-age spear. A roughly worked head at the top designed to mimic sharpened flint. It was bound with leather to the wooden shaft, with a resin in the flinthead's groove where the shaft could sit. It looked rough and well used; it even had a musty smell to it.

Noah's eyes deadened; his mind ripped through his fingers like the others. Sliced, sectioned and put back together, his mind felt examined at the microscopic level. All the joys and pain of his life laid bare.

I've played far too many games and watched too many films for my own good!

Noah slotted in the metal square containing his copied life. He marvelled as the spear transformed in his hand to his *weapon of choice*. On the firing range he'd used sniper rifles a few times as part of his Phase Two training and showed enough ability to hit the target but never enough aptitude to be considered for a marksman role in the squad. *However.*

"That what I think it is?" asked Finn.

"Yep, if you think it's an armour-piercing sniper rifle then you would be spot on. AW50F, half-inch calibre rounds. If I hit something with it, it'll stay hit."

"That's got to be over 30 pounds in weight, 15 kilos," said Lumu, cautiously eyeing Noah's choice. "It'll slow you down."

Noah gave a grim smile, pleased with his choice but knowing the circumstance they were in. He lifted the rifle above his head with his uninjured arm. He'd listened to Smith's account. Lumu's raised eyebrows were enough affirmation for them all.

"I'll be fine."

"Okay, we need to get moving," Finn reached for the last plaque with trepidation. He had admired Lumu's stance; a man of conviction was something he could relate to. But he didn't want to relive everything he'd been through–the worst of it haunted his dreams every night. So many days the panic rose its head when daily life piled on the stress, crippling him at times. Finn knew that his PTSD couldn't match the trauma many went through, he was luckier than so many sufferers. But despite Zuri's demands that he should see a doctor he'd avoided medical help like the plague. His greatest fear was being forced to step back through those burning fires that raged in his mind. What if he never came back out?

Zuri watched Finn's hand tremble as it reached for the plaque. The process had stripped her emotions raw and put her back together again more whole than she'd ever been. Despite reliving her suicide attempt as a teenager, she knew how far she had come since those dark days. The discipline of gymnastic training, followed by that of army life, had enabled her to make sense from the chaos she felt then. Yeah, she could shift emotions like flicking a switch. But Zuri was comfortable with who she was, and who she could be if they made it through the day. But Finn? Would he cope with reliving his nightmare again?

Will he come out the other end at all?

Zuri watched the fire in Finn's eyes dim, unaware she was holding her breath. As they reignited, she searched for any sign he was lost. Finn caught her watching, the amused smile he gave sent relief tingling through her body.

Finn gave Zuri a brief nod, knowing full well what she was searching for. What Finn was searching for himself. How did he feel now? He pushed all the emotions away, sealing them behind a wall of resolve. Whatever the outcome, he was back, and relieved to be there for his squad.

Deal with all that later.

He picked up the strange contraption that was left. A cross between a slingshot and a recurved composite bow he could not make head nor tail of. Whatever, it didn't matter as he placed the square in the grip. The transformation was amazing to watch as the materials ebbed and flowed into his *weapon of choice*. Not the same imagination that Noah had shown but he was comfortable with his selection. Squad complete, he felt the heft of the general purpose machine gun, the ever-reliable L7A2 every squad had used for years. It belied belief, but it weighed no more than his usual assault rifle. The ammunition was going to be an issue, though Smith was adamant they shouldn't worry about it.

Chapter 46

Finn led the way, his mind reeling at what was happening to him. After Zuri had bandaged Noah's arm, Lumu had formed them into buddy teams, insisting on calling them a troop rather than a squad. He had let that go; not an issue. Mills had been sent on his way when Smith opened the main door, Lumu insisting he took an assault rifle with him. No issue there, though it limited Lumu's ammunition. That left the Glocks in the hands of Noah and Lumu, that made sense. Noah needed a short range back up; Lumu was likely to be the last one standing.

Oh no, they weren't the problem. The problem filtered through the helmet radio right now: *Smith.* Before they had left, Smith had insisted he was the only one who knew the location of the ship. That they were operating at night. That no GPS systems or any electronic equipment would work due to the EMP. That only he could make sure they caught up with the alien squad in time. And above all else, it was his duty as a member of the British army and this infantry squad.

"Are you listening to me, Finn, or daydreaming?"

Finn sighed and tapped the metal plaque at the back of his helmet. "This thing glued on? Chance it might accidentally fall off any time soon? It's dark, I might not find it."

"Fat chance of that; I decide when it comes off. And you need me, Finn. Fallen tree ahead, lead the troop to the left five yards to achieve minimal loss of time,"

"How are you doing that, anyway? You're a computer programme stuck to

124

my helmet."

"*The helmet you're wearing is one of the weapons from the House. When I was k —... Sorry. When my body was killed, the copy algorithm took the most likely action to ensure survival. In this case it used what residual energy it had left to transform into a simple helmet after analysing your entry into the airlock. It worked, you took it into the main House, and you know the rest.*"

"Doesn't explain how you are seeing ahead or know where we are going."

"*I recharged when connected to the House AI. I have upgraded your helmet within the limits of the mass I have to play with and the little I have learned about how all this works. As far as I can tell the stronger the connection the weapon has with you over time the more it can eventually do. At the moment it's limited to your knowledge of the weapon, including the subconscious snippets buried in your brain. The mass is an issue, one I haven't got my head around yet, but it's a limiter. As for the helmet, I've adapted it to full spectrum light detection, with radio and sound analysis capabilities all housed in the NV goggles and the PRR. That's what I'm accessing now, as well as reading the ship signal.*"

Finn reached up and slid the Night Vision goggles down. Moving his head in to position, light streams and heat signatures overwhelmed him. The goggles flicked through multiple wavelengths in microseconds. His eyes and brain disagreed with each other instantly as the huge overload hit, and his balance and sense of place wavered. Staggering, and on the border of a sensory shutdown, Finn nudged the goggles quickly back up.

"Okay, I'll let you do that. I'll just point and shoot."

"*Good choice, Lance Corporal.*"

Finn had been paired with Zuri, who shadowed him as they moved through the darkening forest. Corporal Lumu was clearly following procedure in that decision, placing the pairs as near to standard military structure as he could considering the weapons they had chosen. However, Zuri could hear the conflict Lumu faced in his voice and his aversion to look directly at her or Finn when they were together spoke volumes. He clearly found the bond between them difficult, and to be honest, she understood that. Zuri had told Finn as much before their training patrol those few long hours ago. But being back in battle, with them both under the extreme pressure of death and loss once again, had settled that issue for her. They would find a way to be together.

Zuri scanned ahead; dusk was fading into evening and the light was very limited. She could see just fifteen yards where the canopy opened and the light was rapidly dropping further. She understood that Smith, or whatever he was, kept Finn informed about the way ahead. How he was doing it she simply didn't know or want to know. Zuri hadn't the time yet to grieve for so many losses over the last few hours, but she knew losing Smith would hurt immeasurably. They had been firm friends, watching each other's backs across two tours in Afghanistan.

Endure this day, give myself space to grieve. But then me and mine come first.

Chapter 47

Around the room, Vice President Hawlish could feel the tension in the Joint Chiefs of Staff. Normally the room was a hubbub of conversation and even occasional laughter, despite the seriousness of their roles. These men who advised the government on all things military had been the backbone each president relied on. Their decisions saved lives, and America's standing in the world relied on their military knowledge and experience as well as canny political leadership. The pressure of the last few hours had been overwhelming for them and the President, who had been advised to rest as his heart condition reared its ugly head. The room was practically silent, with just the low hum of the surrounding technology. It was not a good sign.

Yet here we are, impotent in the face of an extra-terrestrial threat we all took as an impossibility. If it had landed on our soil, we would have a say, but right now our options are limited.

"Gentlemen, I have spoken with the British ambassador at length. It appears your description of events so far have been accurate, and the ambassador has been open and honest about the situation on the ground. They have found the alien aircraft and strongly believe that each of those jetwings contained an alien. They shed the craft after one of them had been hit and made way on foot back to a Field Camp for the Brit army reserve training where they carried out an armed assault."

The mood in the room shifted noticeably. These were military men; they knew that reserve training would have meant no live ammunition in the field and limited amounts in Field Command itself. It would have been a slaughter.

"The reports from survivors show a pursuit of the aliens by an infantry reserve squad into the forest. An SAS reserve troop has gone in to find them. The UK still has no known objective or motive for this attack." Hawlish took a deep breath as he finished. Grim looks were set across the room.

"Vice President Hawlish, we have reports from our UK and US joint intelligence and communications base in the north of England. They have picked up an EMP pulse knocking out radio and electronic systems around that area." Hawlish nodded at the news from General Brown. He knew enough about electromagnetic pulses to know it should be a minimal threat considering the amount of the military budget spent on shielding against it.

"Sir, these pulses keep repeating and they're in multi-wave form. The techs say it's knocking out most, if not all, electronic systems. Radio traffic in that area is a blind spot, we are getting reports that a transport helicopter has been downed." Hawlish tried to work through the implications. For any military action in the future, this weapon would cause mayhem.

If we are facing an invasion, then God help us all.

"This seriously limits their options for rescue or a strike," the general continued. "Getting soldiers on the ground would normally involve helicopter transport. There is an option if they can find the effective range to drop them in via parachute but then we are talking about navigating a thick tree canopy. Accurate missile strikes need electronic guidance systems, and they have men on the ground with no way of knowing their location. The risk of friendly fire is huge." Brown drew in a long breath. "These reserves are on their own until that pulse ends."

The mood in the Situation Room switched from grim to shocked. Every Chief of Staff understood the impact of the EMP weapon on their own forces. The news was shocking enough for the Brits under fire, but for the world the implications were huge.

"Vice President, we need to make it priority number one that we get hold of as much of the alien technology as we can," spoke up General Marks. "That means not only working with the Brits to overcome this menace but also making absolutely sure none of this technology falls into the wrong hands."

"What about the incoming spaceship? You said if it survived landfall would be up north."

"China has launched, sir. No chance of intercept on our part. Even if there was, politically..." General Marks left the sentence hanging. Everyone knew what interference would lead to.

"Okay, contact our NATO allies and I'll put in calls to the UK government. Draw up plans for blanket coverage by land, sea and air of the area ASAP. And gentlemen," Hawlish scanned the room, displaying outwardly the confidence of government these men needed, "This is a turning point in the history of humanity. Have no doubt the world will never be the same again. Let's make sure we are at the helm."

Chapter 48

Garshellach Forest, nr Stirling
16:16 GMT / 11:16 EST

"Finn, I detect drones ahead," Smith's voice crackled through the radio.

"Can't we just go round? I don't want to go through those bloody seizures all over again. Drool is not a good look."

"Going round will delay us a good five to ten minutes. They've strung four across the route as the forest thickens to the left and right. These guys know exactly what they're doing. It's a trap that you can't bypass without a big delay."

Finn signalled a halt, calling up Corporal Lumu and the rest of the squad, knowing full well there were no hostiles in the immediate area. He quickly repeated what Smith had told him.

"Corporal, these drones have a strobe light. Any flash reaching the retina will incapacitate you with a seizure. The longer you are exposed, the longer you are likely to be out of action. In some cases," Noah looked towards Finn, "it can affect others for longer."

"Options?" asked Lumu.

"We don't know if they have any other weapons capability. If we went through blindfolded and connected someway, we would be sitting ducks. If they don't directly control their drones, they are likely programmed to follow the target." Noah stated, confident in his assessment of the drones' capabilities.

"I can't do anything but track them; it's a shame but I think their dormant heat signature won't be picked up by Zuri's ARILLS sight or we'd be able to take them out from here. I do think we only need to destroy the two in the centre to get by."

Finn relayed what Smith told him.

Zuri hated what she was about to say, but there was no alternative. They had to see this through, and her *weapon of choice* would do the job.

"I have an idea," she grimaced at Finn, mouthing *sorry* before she continued, "Finn goes in blindfolded; Smith directs him, however he does it. When Finn triggers the drone, I take it out. We work our way through the woods until clear. The gunshots will be loud and so a warning to the aliens, but needs must."

"Do it," ordered Lumu, handing his Glock to Finn and taking the unwieldy GPMG in return.

Finn's eyes widened and twitched at the thought of Zuri's plan. It was quick and logical, but it didn't make him feel much better. He recalled little of what happened to him with the drone, but his body lurched at the thought of what he was about to do. At least Zuri hadn't suggested Noah take them out with that cannon he'd chosen. He had visions of the hole it would leave in him if he missed. Taking off his helmet, he accepted the strip of cloth Zuri had taken from the pouches at her hip.

"This clean?"

"Wiped my nose on it just before I gave it to you," Zuri smirked, knowing full well she had placed Finn in a precarious situation once again. "Hit the floor as soon as it's triggered. I won't miss."

"I know. And if you do, well, chances are you might hit Smith." Finn tapped the plaque on the back of his helmet. "Be a shame to stop all the incessant orders he's been giving me."

"Hey. It's the first time you've actually done what you are told, Lance Corporal. I'll make a soldier of you yet."

Finn gave Zuri a brief nod, turned to face the direction Smith indicated and wrapped the cloth around his eyes. Lumu's Glock pistol in hand, he stalked out at pace until Smith told him to slow down. Behind him Zuri had taken a position, with her elbow resting on a broken tree stump for careful balance. She could track Finn's heat signature through the vegetation well enough but was worried about the prospective sound of the gunfire. Finn was going to be in trouble if the aliens came back.

Focus, breathe slow, calm the heart.

To her left Noah had his huge rifle in position, peering through the sight in Finn's direction as the sniper stand kept the muzzle steady. Lumu was by his side, adjusting Noah's hand and arm positions and talking him through posture and breathing. Noah was listening intently, safety most definitely on.

Finn slowed his pace down to careful steps, adjusting his movements as Smith directed him up and over the forest litter and under overhanging branches. It was tough going and he wasn't convinced it was any quicker than going round, time standing still as he focussed on his movements.

"Okay, Finn, I think the next step will trigger the drone. It's slightly to the left of you."

Finn nodded, not daring to talk and hoping Smith could feel it. Finn had no recall of the drone triggering last time, and Smith hadn't encountered the damn things. Mentally he crossed his fingers. Checking his balance, he made the step.

Immediately the drone rose in the air, Finn's sense of the movement warned him though it made an imperceptible amount of noise.

" Down, Finn."

He hit the floor.

As soon as Finn made the last step Zuri caught the new heat signature to the left. It was tiny compared to Finn's, but clear. In that moment Zuri wished it was bigger, that she was a better shot, that she could strike before the drone moved and the thermal images blurred together. The sight self-adjusted, arrowing on to the smaller heat signature, cross hairs dead centre. Smooth as silk, Zuri pulled the trigger and a near silent trace of heat smashed into the drone; it shuddered and separated into a myriad of briefly flaring images. Zuri breathed in, relief washing through her. She rubbed at her eyes, trying not to think about the weapon she held despite her gratitude. It had adapted that shot, giving her the clearest target and silencing the sound. On this crazy day it was the least of her worries.

Now for the next one.

Chapter 49

Approaching Field Command, Garshellach Forest
16:20 GMT / 11:20 EST

Trooper Mills winced as he stumbled over the protruding root. The painkillers Zuri had given him took the edge off initially but right now as he scrambled through the forest, he was not so sure they were doing anything. Every breath pressed against his sore ribs and the resultant sharp pain response forced it back out. Mills knew very well those quick breaths were affecting his ability to maintain pace and that he'd suffer for it in the long run. However, if he was to achieve his long-term goal of being in the full SAS, then he had to see it through. Mills had joined as a volunteer in the infantry reserve initially, but the army had quickly seen his potential and encouraged him to join up fully. His family life stopped that from happening; his children had needed him at home and his electrician job paid the bills. When they'd fast-tracked him into the SAS reserve he'd thrived, his electrical knowledge being a boon too. Mills had completed one tour alongside the full SAS and he was sold. His wife now saw the need in him, and was proud, to be honest. They'd get through it.

Mills shifted the strange rifle on his back to a more comfortable position, then regretted the sudden movement as agony scoured his chest. He regretted agreeing to take back some of the alien tech, but Corporal Lumu had been adamant it was vital and part of their orders to secure what they could. The alien belt across his chest added weight too but dropping his body armour had helped there. Not a choice he enjoyed making but needs must, and it helped him breathe just a little easier.

The route back was less demanding to follow than he'd expected. His night vision goggles were useless with the EMP still active but Mills could retrace the route taken by his squad. Remembering where and when most of the major obstacles came up was a great help. Overall, he was making good time despite his injury.

Mills caught a movement in the corner of his eye. At first it was flickering in and out, but as he walked a little closer, it resolved into a distant light source. Corporal Lumu had insisted he take the assault rifle and right now he was glad of it. Ahead, as his own night vision adjusted; he could see a small flame in the tree line. Amongst the damp wood and vegetation of the forest any fire was unlikely to be natural. Not being able to maintain the crouch because of the pain, Mills moved along, keeping the fire to his right as he progressed.

Do I stay on mission? If it's more aliens, then I'm screwed. If it's ours, then I may get out of here quicker.

He moved into the thicker undergrowth cautiously with his ribs giving sharp reminders to take care. As he crept closer, Mills could see the flame coming from within the tree canopy. The light bounced amongst the branches, and he made out a broken rotor. Mills upped his pace to an urgent but painful level, recognising the markings and insignia along the helicopter's tail. Mills scanned the area, then flanked the left and round the back. Satisfied there were no hostiles he moved in, eyes roaming as he searched for the crew.

The helicopter had fallen through the trees, its tail pitched against a fir with the rotor aflame, but Mills knew his electrics. No worries there, probably a short burning out. The tail had cracked and split. The cockpit rested on a broken tree trunk but there was no fuel smell, just a tumble of internal wiring systems laid bare. Mills moved around the split trunk to be met by the gunner. He'd not known his name, an anonymous trainer from his SAS reserve operation that day. A branch protruded from his thigh; the artery likely severely damaged though the blood splatter was minimal. His broken, rag doll body lay with the neck at an unnatural angle. Mills moved on; duty first.

The side door remained open, Mills suspected it had been all along with the gunnery position manned. He glanced inside; the cockpit was in one piece and both seats were empty. A small blood trail with partial boot prints through it led outwards. Mills scanned for and found the signs of someone being dragged through the vegetation and followed, his ribs reminding him they were still there. As he moved around a leafy bush Mills caught partial sight of a figure kneeling behind a tree, his hands clearly working at something. The flight suit gave him hope.

"SAS Trooper Mills," he called. "Here to help."

And don't shoot me.

The figure leaned back and looked his way, the glow of the flames lighting up his face. It was Jenkins, the Pilot Officer with a desperate look on his face. Jenkins followed procedure, calling out his name and rank. Mills approached and knelt next to the man, with his bruised and battered Flying Officer lent against the tree bleeding profusely from a neck wound.

"I can't stop it. He needs medical attention ASAP. His pulse is slowing," Jenks said, agitation and stress running through his voice. His hands pressing on the wound.

Mills took a large patch from his kit, a haemostatic gauze. He balled one part and pushed it under Jenk s' hands and into the wound. Without direction Jenks pressed down. Mills continued to press the gauze in to the wound, with Jenks reapplying the pressure after each one.

"Any other wounds I need to be aware of?" Mills asked as they worked.

"Not on first assessment, none that I can see are life threatening," said Jenks. "I likely have a broken ankle, but I'll survive."

Mills nodded. Coming to the end of his first pack, he assessed the impact. Blood still seeped through the gauze as he examined the edges around Jenkin's hand. The cut was deep and the bandage was not yet above the wound lip. He opened the last pack and started again.

"Any radio working?"

"Not tried it, but most of the electronics were affected by the EMP that kept repeating. It's what took us out of the sky. The systems couldn't cope." The Flying Officer winced as he shifted his ankle.

Mills nodded, aware that his options were severely limited and there was a life at stake. As he came to the end of the gauze, he could see that the blood had not stopped.

"Hold it for at least three minutes. I'll be back."

I need to try the radio. That pulse may have passed, and I need this man out of here ASAP. If the radio shorts out, then I know not to use mine.

Mills clambered through the door and sat in the pilot's seat. He checked the systems over—no power, and nor did he want to engage anything with possible ruptured tanks. Not with shorting electrics and whatever missiles this bird was carrying. The risk was low, system fail-safes were damn good but who knew what effect this EMP had on them.

He quickly checked the radio console: dead, no power. Swiftly taking out his toolkit, Mills worked at the console, eventually extracting a section and removing two sets of wires. Spinning his belt pack round, he pulled out the small PRR pack linked to his helmet. He extracted the battery pack. Within a minute, he had it wired up.

C'mon, work. Just need a little juice.

Mills flicked the switch on the radio. Static crackled and he could hear a low hum followed by a few faint movements in the radio waves. He waited for the radio to short, if the EMP was still active he reckoned it was on a ten second cycle. He gave it fifteen, and nothing changed.

Time for a risk.

Mills switched the battery back into his PRR. The UK Bowman communication system was an unwieldy beast but the SAS troop had access through their radios unlike many other army units. At least Corporal Lumu did, and this was his set.

As Lumu's radio came to life, Mills let out a pained sigh.

"This is SAS 23, D Air Trooper Mills on Corporal Lumu's PRR. We need immediate pick up. I repeat —"

"UK Special Forces command receiving, Trooper Mills."

Chapter 50

Garshellach Forest, nr Stirling
16:25 GMT / 11:25 EST

Finn crouched, raised his arm to signal a halt and waited. Smith had asked for a pause whilst he analysed the visual sensory data coming in. They had destroyed the second drone the same way as the first. Zuri had made good on her promise, her aim was true. They'd not spoken since, returning to their buddy team as they moved on and keeping to their expected silence as much as they could. Finn had kept the makeshift blindfold round his neck just in case.

It was a relief to get past the drones without incident, but Finn had a strong feeling that the new aliens were better trained and more capable. Their attack from the rear on Corporal Lumu's troop had been carefully coordinated, their use of the EMP weapon logical and well-timed to reduce communication and support. With all their technology Finn couldn't understand why that first contact group had been so belligerent. They could easily have bypassed Field Command and entered the woods with little pursuit. And what about the alien they found first off, his throat slashed by his own commander? It was almost as if they wanted to test themselves.

Or maybe just one of them did.

"Finn, the spaceship is about 100 yards ahead according to the readings. It's underground, about five feet down. On thermal I can just make out four alien signatures approaching the area, matching those we've seen earlier. They are very faint, I wonder if they have some form of shielding up. Not sure if Noah will be able to pick any out with his thermal sight."

137

"What about us, Smith? I'm guessing they'll be able to pick us out pretty soon, even with the trees."

"I think I can scatter your thermal signature, Finn; it won't be invisible to my sensors but it's the best I can do. I can do nothing about the others."

Finn signalled Lumu and Noah forward, moving off the path to a pile of ancient volcanic rocks that would block some of their heat signature. He detailed what Smith had told him.

"So, if they follow the previous operational procedure the two technicians will approach the ship and attempt entry whilst the two others guard. They'll likely scatter drones if they have any left along obvious routes in." Zuri and Finn nodded along with Lumu's assessment.

"The activation range on the drones is around eight to ten feet at the maximum, but it doesn't give much time to react," Zuri added.

"And we have no PRR capability between us, so any attack has to be coordinated by timing and visual signal if we get close. That means it's Zuri, Finn and me on close contact. Noah, you will need to keep out of the main combat, whatever happens. I can't risk a wrong decision in there. Hope that cannon works." Noah nodded at Corporal Lumu's words.

"If I may, Corporal," Finn said, " I can take a position say sixty-five to seventy yards from the target point if Smith's assessment is correct about scattering my thermal image. I can provide suppressing fire from there. If things go wrong, I can provide support on retreat." Zuri eyed Finn for a moment, thinking through his idea. Normally Finn would want to be leading any combat, but he was right. The weapon he'd chosen was a wise one to support the fireteam. He was also accepting what was coming next, not that he had a choice.

"Right, Noah takes up position here. Check for eyes on target. Finn, you take position as you suggested to the right in the best cover you can find. Zuri and I will take a position at one hundred yards on the right and left flanks. Zuri, keep eyes on with that nightscope of yours. Noah, check if you have a target, preferably a guard. On his shot, Finn, you lay the suppressing fire. Zuri drops in one grenade and we then both go in hard and fast. This is on timing, so if Noah has not taken that shot, say, by four minutes time on my mark, then Zuri, you take the first shot with that scope of yours. Agreed?" Lumu scanned the soldiers for a response.

"And the drones?" asked Noah.

"If you're hit with a drone before Noah's shot then we act–no choice as we'll be seen. If one of us gets strobed on the way in, so be it. The rest carry through the mission, *whoever* it is." Lumu gazed at Zuri, making sure his message was understood. She nodded.

Noah took up the position behind the rocks, then checked his watch against the rest of the squad's.

"Mark," stated Lumu, and they all moved. Noah set his quiet alarm just in case.

Noah settled his nerves as he worked through the checklist Corporal Lumu had set for him. First, he focussed on calming his breathing and heartbeat. With deliberate care he adjusted the bipod on the rock so he could rest his arms in a comfortable position. Three minutes in one position was a long time. He then rested his cheek against the place on the stock comb Lumu had shown him. Lining up his eye with the sight, he tweaked his shoulder and neck to readjust that position.

Now calm the breathing again; remember we shoot on the breath pause, just before breathing in.

Noah peered through the sight, searching for the four thermal images. There were very faint signatures, difficult to make out as they moved in and out of focus. Noah concentrated, noting a pair move next to each other before kneeling, the brief glow of an object in each of their hands. He scanned left but couldn't see any guard on that side, and then right to be met by a brief flicker of an image. Possibly this one was a target, but a high-risk one.

That's a minute gone, I have time.

Finn had moved forward, crouching low to double up on Smith's promised disruption of his thermal image. He eyed the vegetation around him and, after twenty yards, slipped into the undergrowth, seeking a suitable position. The chances of finding the perfect rock or stone were slim, but he hoped to find something where he could stabilise the machine gun with a sweeping view of the aliens.

"Remember, once you fire, no thermal image dispersal will hide you," whispered Smith in his ear. *"Need you alive, Finn, I don't want to spend the rest of my days upside down as a bird's nest."*

Finn ignored Smith as he tried to keep his feet from snapping any debris. Half of his mind worried about the drones, the other half about the task ahead. He suppressed his fears about Zuri; that would do no one any good. Finn then came across a rotten tree trunk at chest height laying roughly parallel with the target.

There, that'll do. Little protection from return fire but it's the best I can do. Two minutes to go.

Zuri moved through the undergrowth and between the low-branched trees with care. She had time, Lumu had ensured a balance between speed and caution. If they were discovered now when out of position, they'd be ripped apart. She knew well enough the power of some of their weapons, including those seizure-inducing drones. Zuri had spotted Finn had left his blindfold around his neck and copied his choice, using an arm sling from her First Aid kit.

Having travelled diagonally towards her designated area, Zuri continued to step with care. She began to pause and take the occasional check through her own thermal sight to ensure she wasn't too far, or near, to her designated position. Zuri was acutely aware she had to get as much cover as possible. Getting too close would make her a target. When she reached a point she favoured, she crouched, ready.

One minute to go, hope Noah's ready.

Lumu ducked behind the pile of fallen branches, eyes forward, scanning the target as best he could in the dark. After all the years spent in the Gurkha regiment, and later the SAS, and now their reserves, his experience was hard to match. But here and now he would happily trade it all for a moment of clarity in the madness of the last few hours. He had lost two of his troop to aliens, intent unknown. Their capabilities were not that far advanced, just enough to maintain a constant edge over them, but not so much that they didn't have some sliver of a chance. However, he was taking advice from a computer programme claiming to be a dead corporal and leading half a squad, including a rookie who hadn't passed their final phase of training. This incarnation was proving taxing; he just hoped he had been true to his path.

Thirty Seconds.

Chapter 51

Noah had his target. The guards' images were inconsistent, the variation too risky. He knew he had to take out a technician, no choice. But just as he settled on which one, a steady shadow of heat blossomed at the technicians' feet. Initially this was low level, in one defined spot. But the signature quickly developed and spread across the entire area. It swiftly blurred and merged with the technicians' images and Noah lost his shot.

No, no, no. It can't be.

His watch alarm vibrated; Noah felt the panic rise in his stomach. He had to keep calm, manage his nerves. But as he yearned for the images to sharpen the scope reacted and focussed in. The image heat levels redefined, his target's shadow oh so slightly colder against the rising background heat. Noah squeezed the trigger on his pause of breath, the shot released left no muzzle flash as it drove towards the target.

Finn watched the forest floor lift in front of him, a glow from under the ground seeping through the soil and brightening the area in front of him. The ground rumbled; he felt the thrum through his boots. Vibrations forced the rocks to jump and dance and the forest floor at the technicians' feet began to rise and separate.

"It's the ship. They've activated the radio link to bring it up," said Smith.

Then Noah's shot rang out, clear above the rumble of earth and rock being stretched and ripped asunder. It struck the alien stumbling from the rising ship in the lower abdomen plate, sending him backward towards the rising tide. Finn could see the ceramic plate shatter as the high-calibre shot hit home but could not confirm any more. He let loose.

Zuri gaped, open-mouthed as the ground lifted before her eyes. The glow had blinded her rifle sight, rendering her unaware of what was happening. But that wasn't her primary objective, she knew her job and the distance required.

Pull yourself together, woman.

Zuri sent the grenade on her way, took a breath and moved forward at pace, Finn's machine gun fire adding to the sensory mix of noise, movement and sudden light. After thirty yards she stopped briefly behind cover, checking the launcher and sending a grenade blindly into the maelstrom, knowing full well none of her squad would be there yet.

Onward.

Corporal Lumu had launched himself forward as Noah's shot reached its target; time was of the essence. But he needed to stay out of the sweep of Finn's suppressing fire. Keeping low he jumped and wove his way through the underbrush, his movement improved by the increasing glow around him. It wasn't until he was nearly halfway that his brain recognised the change, the light that broke through the murk, the rumble beneath his feet and the sound of the earth tearing ahead of him. He came to a halt, crouching and aiming towards the target. Lumu took a quick look through the rifle's day sight, still attached from the military exercise, assessed the events before him and breathed out.

He ignored the spaceship lifting itself from the ground but took in the devastation caused by grenade and bullet. One technician down, struggling to get up, with a hole in his stomach. The other prone but moving towards the guard on Lumu's side of the attack. Before the alien guard stood a metal shield made of interlocking plates from a central hub. Its edges shimmered in the new light; bullets hammered into the shield from Finn's machine gun before he swept over to the other side.

Damn.

As Finn's suppressing fire moved on, he noted the guard on the far side, his back peppered with shrapnel but still standing. Again, Finn's bursts rattled

143

against the metal as he kept the guard at bay.

Lumu desperately wished for his radio; now was the time for Zuri and him to hit the guards from the side, pepper their exposed legs; they'd have had to react eventually if they outflanked them. It needed to be now; he knew Finn's barrel would overheat soon.

It was then that a second grenade landed directly in front of the shielded guard on Zuri's side. The shrapnel shredded the metal, the explosive force sending the alien careering backwards. Lumu immediately fired upon the guard nearest him, spraying a burst along the leg armour.

Finn watched the second grenade launch the guard backwards behind a growing pile of earth and rocks. The spaceship loomed above the scene, perhaps twenty yards high and a hundred yards wide, with more to come. It was smooth, a blueish lustre to the curved metal. No mud or rock clung to its surface which seemed to shine with promised power. He did his best to ignore it, focussing on the job at hand. He needed to reduce the bursts. The hot slugs would soon render the barrel inoperable, though he could feel no heat or glow from the muzzle. Finn was switching targets as the rotten wood in front of him splintered and shattered under a barrage of fire. The wooden shards hammered into his combat armour; he'd hit the deck before it showered towards his neck and head.

"Close one, Finn. That was the second technician, they've got a good aim. The one Noah hit is still alive, how I don't know. His heat signature is steady. Must have a cast iron stomach."

Finn picked up his GPMG and sped towards the middle pathway, away from Zuri, but he needed a full arc if he was to be of any help. He weaved through the bushes and low vegetation, desperate to find a useful placement.

As Finn moved, Zuri reached the line of sight to the far guard and technician on Lumu's flank. Her guard was nowhere to be seen though the pitted metal shield lay where she thought he should be. The ship was still rising, and the pile of rock and mud around it was a potential hiding place. Zuri raised her rifle to target Lumu's alien when the drone rose from the vibrating forest floor to her left. Simultaneously, her guard rolled out from the rockpile shooting fizzing bursts of energy as he did so from his sidearm.

No!

Chapter 52

"Returning to base, we have three–I repeat, three–survivors aboard. Flying Officer Ibrahim needs urgent medical treatment. Please advise command." Flying Officer Marshall clicked off, awaiting his orders. Ibrahim was touch and go; they needed direction. This had been a training exercise, not a full set of manoeuvres. There was no field hospital and Ibrahim urgently needed specialist treatment.

"Head for Stirling, Wildcat Two. We will notify ahead and clear a space to land," came the notification back. Marshall breathed a heavy sigh of relief. With the craziness of this day, he had half expected something else. "Can you put Trooper Mills on, please, secure channel."

Marshall looked over to the trooper gingerly holding his ribs in the back. The man had been through it, but showed a clear head and mind. Without him he doubted Ibrahim would have had any chance. He waved over to the gunner, signalling to pass on his radio. With a thumbs up, he complied. Mills took the headset and settled in for his expected long debrief. The joys of covert ops.

These ribs are killing me.

"Trooper Mill —" he reported, but stopped as the gunner's agitated pointing through the open side door caught his attention. In the distance a blue object was peeking above the ridge line, slowly rising. Disorientated amongst the mayhem of rescue, he couldn't say for certain it was where Corporal Lumu had been heading, but then again, why wouldn't it be? He estimated it was

146

about two miles distant, making it almost the size of a…

Oh, wow, that's going to be fun to explain.

Chapter 53

Garshellach Forest, nr Stirling
16:36 GMT / 11:36 EST

Noah's crosshairs blurred and flared as the thermal levels made it impossible to use, the image dissipating in a glare of white heat. As the sight adjusted, the image crystallised and focussed on the area in front of the ship. Sharp, defined; he had Zuri within his vision. Between her and him the drone hovered, threatening. No time. Zuri hit the floor, hard.

The shot rang out, a crack loud and powerful echoing against the rising wall of rock and earth. It slid by the drone, missing by a whisker as it slammed into the spaceship behind, ricocheting off harmlessly.

As the guard brought his roll to a stop Zuri released a burst of rifle fire into his mask, releasing a second and third with a little less accuracy as the pain in her side grew. The bullets battered and cracked the ceramic shell at the top of the mask, raking their way through the gel beneath. The third burst, shredding what was beneath as the guard died.

Zuri threw herself on to her side as the whirr of the strobe started, knowing full well she'd be too late. Then a second round from Noah smashed into the metal casing and the drone disintegrated as the explosive penetrated through to its inner workings.

Mwenye kutenda jamala, naye hulipwa jamala. To the person who does kind things, kind things will be done. I owe you one, Noah.

Zuri felt inside her combat armour, the alien's energy bolt had burned through the armour and on into her flesh. No blood, no pain around her organs, but it hurt like hell.

Lumu spared Zuri a glance through his scope as she checked her wound, relieved that she was still moving though he did not know how. The alien's joint attack had been cleverly planned, the drone acting on command. He returned his aim to the guard nearest to him, sending in shortened bursts to keep him at bay. The technician moved out to his left, the guard's right, and the corporal knew full well he was planning to flank him. His serious lack of ammo heightened the problem; one more burst and he would be down to the Glock pistol at his hip.

Time to move.

As Lumu sent his final burst slamming into the armoured leg and metal shield, Finn's GPMG erupted back into the affray. Lumu had assumed the alien response after Finn's initial assault had seriously wounded or even killed him. Somewhat heartened, he let the rifle drop. Slipping the Glock into his hand Lumu moved cautiously towards where he expected the technician to be.

In normal circumstances, Zuri would not have remotely considered the use of a grenade at such close quarters. But injured, with two well-armed aliens on the loose, she accepted the risk. She checked the launcher to once again find a newly installed grenade in place. Being careful to ensure the grenade landed this side of the guard and the edge of his metal shield, Zuri let fly, then dived behind the earth mound her assailant had come from, rolling forward and slamming against the side of the now-motionless blue-metalled spaceship.

Chapter 54

Spaceship, Garshellach Forest
16:38 GMT / 11:38 EST

Zuri placed her left her hand against the spaceship as she tried to regain her composure. The pain in her side reminded her it was still there, her head ringing despite the standard-issue helmet taking the brunt of the impact against the metal carcass of the spaceship.

Immediately she felt a warmth spread through her hand. She pulled it back, but her hand felt sucked on to the metal like a limpet. Dropping her assault rifle in panic, she pulled harder; the anxiety overriding the consequences of what she was doing. Hot needles slid in her palm, and deeper into her hand and wrist. Zuri was conscious of the blood flowing out from her; she wanted to keep every precious drop.

No, no, no, no. No!

After a few seconds struggle, her palm moistened, the skin sliding from her palm and remaining on the metalled wall as she pulled back. Zuri's mind flipped as the skin cells absorbed into the metal. She stared at the spot, scrabbling at the metal to get that precious part of her back. The outer skin of the spaceship altered, an outline of a doorway edge defining in front of her eyes. The gentle motor stirred, and the door opened. A sudden rush of movement and a slam in her back forced her through. Her *weapon of choice* dropped to the floor — on the outside.

Chapter 55

Garshellach Forest
16:38 GMT / 11:38 EST

Lumu stalked through the undergrowth, glad of the light and heat bathing the forest and negating the use of any imaging. The pistol low in the ready position, he moved through the bushes and trees with his eyes and ears tuning in to his surroundings. He knew Finn had dropped his rate of fire, but he hoped to be alive to deal with that later.

A crack of a branch ahead brought him to a standstill. Eyes adjusting, he caught a strange outline against the branches through the next line of trees. To Lumu's senses, brought up in the mountains and forests of Nepal, it did not sit right. Lumu moved his head to look away; side-eyeing the same space, he took another step, watching warily. An unnatural movement of the branch followed, the ripple through the branches setting his nerves on edge. Raising his Glock to aim forward, he spun low and downwards, bringing his right arm round to bear upon the tree. He fired before he landed on his right side, firing again for the mask as the alien moved and lost its camouflage advantage. Both shots hit home, the first hitting the groin plate and rebounding off into the woods, the second striking the respirator intake and driving the mask back in to the alien's face.

The alien, bringing the rifle to bear, lost its aim and direction as the second bullet smashed into its mask. The projectile missed by inches, striking a trunk over Lumu's head. He heard the explosion soon followed by a more worrying burst of heat and the eruption of splintered wood, which rained against his combat armour. Lumu scrambled to his feet, diving forwards as the tree came crashing down towards him. A second shot drilled into the ground at his feet, the eruption behind him blasting soil and stone into the air.

He's using something slow and powerful, maybe not so combat trained as the guards. I hope.

Lumu weaved through the trees as the third shot rang out, drilling through the branches in front of him and on into the ground. This time the spray erupted across his path, causing him to stumble and fall into the dirt. This wasn't going so well.

Chapter 56

Garshellach Forest
16:39 GMT / 11:39 EST

Finn had not seen the danger Zuri was in before Noah's intervention as he dodged through the undergrowth, seeking a place where he could set back up with a full sweep of the battleground. On finding it he had kicked back in, slamming rounds in to the one guard's shield he could see. When Zuri had emerged, firing her grenade and diving towards the ship, he breathed a sigh of relief that she still stood, despite her labouring movements favouring one side. But as she disappeared over the mound the grenade hardly scarred the alien's armour. Pitted in places, it took the blast with no crack or fissure in the ceramic plates.

Come to think of it, Finn noted his own bullets as they clattered against the metal shield, the odd one or two clipping the armour of his target. The impacts were lessening; the effects reducing strike by strike.

"Smith, what's happening to the weapons? The impact of the rounds is dropping."

"They are running out of juice, Finn. The amount of power is finite. I told you the more you connect with the weapons the more powerful they will be. Think of it like memory: the more you learn and use something the more of it you retain. The weapons are like that; keep using the same weapons and the links strengthen as it understands what you want. Also, the more powerful the weapon you want, the less usage you will get. I estimate you have around eight more three-round bursts before your weapon is fully discharged." Smith paused, analysing, then said, *"Lumu is facing off against the other technician. I'd say he's in trouble, Finn, but*

we've got this guy to deal with. And Zuri... oh. Oh, no."

"Spill it, Smith," shouted Finn down the PRR. His patience with his squad leader wearing thinner by the second.

"Zuri... Zuri's off my sensors. Gone, as is the wounded technician. The one Noah struck at the beginning of the assault." Smith sounded truly lost, shocked.

"She was just there, Smith. Against the ship. I watched her roll out after sending the grenade. Check again." Tension ripped through Finn, but he maintained the slow bursts to pin the guard.

"No sign, Finn. I think she's in the ship."

"Think or know, Smith? It's important."

"With no other possibility it's the only one left. She's in the ship, and the technician with her."

Chapter 57

Garshellach Forest
16:40 GMT / 11:40 EST

Corporal Lumu tried to gain sight of the alien hunting him down. As he'd hit the dirt it had been off to his left, visible after the movement against the trees. He could sense that it had moved on, possibly further to his left.

Either I wait for the killing shot or I mo —

He half-scrambled, half-ran forwards as the single shot rang out, the bullet striking and exploding to his left against a solid target. In his hurry, Lumu could only spare a brief glance to see the alien slamming against a tree, dropping the rifle. A plate at his left shoulder had fractured, a hole drilled through where a mixture of green gel and red blood spurted.

Noah.

Lumu altered his path, raising the Glock as he did so and pumping the rest of the magazine into the armour around the initial wound. Charging onwards, his momentum knocked the creature to the floor, taking him with it. Lumu, agile and strong, landed on top. Pushing his right hand deep in to the wound he reached behind him and pulled out his kukri, the knife of the Gurkhas. He slid the hooked blade between the ceramic plates and slowly pressed down, adding his body weight to increase the pressure through the edge. The black Kevlar-like material parted under the sharp edge. With the kinetic gel unable to dissipate the slowly applied force, the kukri slid off the backplate and on into the flesh and vital organs below.

Awash with the conflicting emotions of taking a life, Lumu missed the low hum of a motor, the press of a trigger, but not the deep fire within his chest as the energy ripped through his combat armour at point blank range. As his heart seared, Lumu gave his last breath for the army with the same bravery and honour that he'd given his first.

Chapter 58

Spaceship, Garshellach Forest
16:42 GMT / 11:42 EST

Zuri landed heavily upon the bronzed, polished floor. The wind knocked out of her, a second impact followed as her assailant's armoured body landed on her lower torso and legs. Pain shot through her side again, bringing her back to her senses. Struggling for a simple breath, Zuri knew she was in desperate trouble.

Must move! Forward? Sideways?

Being fitter than most she would recover quickly, but with her life on the line it wouldn't be quick enough. She tried to heave herself up, clambering along the floor away from whatever was on her legs.

The weight slipped off as she moved, but above the slap of her hands upon the floor and her lungs straining for air Zuri could hear very little. She awaited the inevitable ring of gunfire, or the searing pain of contact as she moved. Surely it would be soon.

Are they just torturing me? I want to live.

Zuri spun on to her side to glance behind her. The alien technician lay on the floor, its arms splayed and four-digit hands empty. The mask lay split and broken on the smooth floor next to the exposed head. Zuri could catch a rise and fall of the body as it breathed, but it was slow and laboured. She slid across the floor. Her mind ran over the killing of the sword-wielding alien earlier in the day. She had never wanted to take a life–in fact, life was more precious to her every day. But when forced, she had no qualms or long-term regrets. She slipped her keen-edged knife from its sheath.

I have not taken a life except to defend me or mine. These have taken life with ruthlessness and anger, armed or not.

Distressed by the lack of air, Zuri cut the weapon holster from the alien's hip. She was in no condition to fight, but this gave her a chance. Zuri knelt up in a crouch, taking the recovery position she used so often in her gymnastics.

Relax. Relax and breathe slow and deep.

As Zuri followed her own instructions, she looked back to the entrance. She just knew it would be closed; the way her day had gone so far it couldn't be anything else. The rest of the room, including the ceiling, bore smooth polished metal, though each was a different hue. She glanced down the room and noted a closed door in the far wall about ten feet away. At the side, a large palm lock glowed with a familiar blue light. To her mind it looked like a security corridor, even an airlock.

Like the House.

As Zuri's breathing returned, she took a long, lingering breath as she considered her options. As she did so, the alien pulled its left arm underneath its body and pushed itself up. Zuri moved gracefully despite her pain into a fighting stance, blade ready. Without the mask Zuri could see the large, inflamed eyes and the pronounced nostrils filled with blood. With its thin lips blue and spiral tattoos, the technician's face appeared like a comically drawn parody of a human male. This would not be a long struggle.

The technician pushed itself further up and against the wall into an awkward sitting position. Blood poured from the wound in its abdomen. If it was human, then Zuri did not give it long before its body gave out.

A series of clicks and harsh words slipped between the blue lips, its eyes seeking Zuri's as it directed the words towards her. The tug of familiarity returned. She didn't know this language, but somewhere, somehow, her subconscious did.

"I don't understand," said Zuri.

And I'm not sure I want to.

The alien's tumbling language became repetitive, but more urgent in tone.

"Please, there's no point. You have come to my planet and attacked us. I don't care. Please just die."

A series of lights flashed above Zuri, grabbing her attention. Patterned shades of blue in the ceiling coalesced into a holographic head, hooded, though the attention was clearly on her.

Zuri's ear drums suddenly vibrated; she could feel the air around her move and a pressure build. She moved her hands to cover her ears but felt the tremble of her muscles and bones as the shaking spread.

"Adjusting... language root origin distant. Adjusting." A robotic voice echoed through the room. The vibrations deep within her ears had stopped as soon as she heard the unfamiliar voice. The technician's eyes had never left her, continuing to plead in clicks and syllables.

"Ah, a civilised language, Khoisan derivative. Let's see..." The disembodied voice shifted to the clicks and harsh sounds the alien was using. The response from the alien was excited but pained, its head nodding in a distinctly human way before launching in to a back-and-forth conversation. Zuri was lost for what to do, time was slipping by and she needed out.

"The Khoisan language is so much more versatile. I have been asked to translate for *!Nais*," Zuri took that as a name, "He is dying, and he knows you can finish him any time. *!Nais* wants you to know that *!ke*, his people, have not come to kill but to take. He apologises for his people but they are desperate, his *!ke* are slowly dying out. This day hurts him to the heart, but they need this ship."

The rage rose from within; the pain and anger at the loss and death over the day fuelled Zuri.

"Loss? They took my commander's life with no provocation. Murdered defenceless rookies. Hurt?" Zuri's knife throbbed in her hand. She rocked back and forth on her feet, trying to contain the storm brewing within her as the hooded voice translated her words.

!Nais let forth a wave of clicks and syllables towards her, one hand raised palm out as the other pressed against his abdomen. His breath bubbled as blood seeped into his lungs.

"*!Nais* says that the first group was 'bad'; that's not the word, but it's the best I can do. They woke from a long sleep of about three hundred years too quickly. They went off mission, one in particular was unstable. When they

159

landed his group were left with no choice but to carry on the mission as they found it. They took no lives other than those that were necessary to reach the... he calls me a 'SeedShip', though that's not my current role. Yet."

The fury had not left Zuri; she had no time or the knowledge to analyse what had happened. She just knew the loss she felt. But information was a weapon of war and right now they needed as much as they could get.

"Why here? Why the SeedShip? Will there be more coming?" she blurted, awaiting the response with trepidation as the voice asked her questions in Khoisan.

"He says this is the... errr... human origin world? That they couldn't access their own SeedShip but broke in when they found it. They had no permission for information access but gained a location for your world before it self-destructed. They need the technology and knowledge on offer to survive."

The alien started to slip away; Zuri could see the life draining from his eyes. She knew he spoke a last few words as his lips moved, but they never reached her ears. She stared at the body, not knowing what to feel as the adrenaline washed through her.

"He said: We are one people, one *!ke*, you and I, we are human. I beg you to help my people survive."

Chapter 59

Garshellach Forest
16:42 GMT / 11:42 EST

Noah peered down the sniper rifle's sight, his eye not wavering from Corporal Lumu. The panic he felt was difficult to control. Lumu wasn't moving, his chest not stirring with the rhythm of breath. It had taken an age for Noah to get a safe shot at the alien, too long. But the camouflage had been perfect from his position and for all the adaptability of the sight it could not identify where it was. By the time he got the shot in they were so close, and Lumu had gone in bravely to finish the fight.

We've lost him.

Noah lifted his head and scanned the area in front of him. The spaceship had stopped rising, it was still and glowing with the light that had rendered his thermal sight useless. The rattle of Finn's machine gun had altered; it now sounded from the left as he faced the ship, and the rate of fire had dropped significantly. By Noah's understanding, only the guard on that side was still operational but his weapon failed to pick him up. It must have shifted under the barrage from Finn and now a rock blocked his view.

Need to go. Find Finn. Need orders.

As he rose from his sniper position, Noah heard the clatter from the machine gun end. Either Finn had taken the last alien hostile down or he was out of ammunition. Noah slipped the awkward rifle into the easiest ready position he could and moved forward. Keeping low, it was most unlikely that either side of this combat could use any enhanced imaging.

I hope.

Finn dropped the L7A2 to the floor, it was spent, and he needed to end this soon. He needed to find Zuri, and nothing was going to get in his way. The alien was in a mess but functioning. The battering of the shield and the rounds that got through had taken a toll. Smith had detailed the shattered armour and the signs of the alien's distress at the constant attack.

"I think Lumu's dead. He's not moving. Looks like he took out the other alien. This is the last one outside of the ship."

Finn winced, Smith's words striking at the fear for Zuri balled deep within him.

"This one will know soon enough that you are out of ammo. He has a decision to make. Does he go for you or for the ship?"

Finn moved towards the left, aiming to check on Lumu and perhaps scavenge a weapon if he could.

"Take the machine gun, Finn. You can't leave it behind."

Finn ignored Smith; he didn't need it getting in the way.

"I order you, Lance Corporal, to retain your weapon."

Finn continued for a step or two, then spun back, taking it by the stock.

He'll only just go on and on about it.

Hot energy seared into the spot he'd just left, shredding the bushes and branches as he moved. The smell of burning leaves and pine needles hit the air. Finn scrabbled back, aiming for a tree to at least give him some cover. The high energy bolts slammed into the trunk, singeing his boot as he brought it up behind him. Finn knew stopping would be his end and sprinted, hoping that he could barge his way through the undergrowth. Crashing through a bare autumnal bush he suddenly came upon Noah, crouched, holding his rifle and taking aim. The shot rang out and Finn grabbed his arm, pulling Noah over as the alien fire crisped the leaves and branches where he had been. They lay flat, waiting.

"Did you hit him?" whispered Finn.

"Yes, but the bullet didn't penetrate that armour. Impact sent him backwards."

"Then move." Finn was up, the machine gun in his hands forgotten as he raced through the woods. Noah was at his heels with no less of an awkward weapon to carry. As they crashed through the woods, Noah directed Finn towards Lumu's body. Panting, they slid behind the alien underneath Lumu, pulling Lumu's body down as they rolled the alien's armoured corpse upwards. Noah brought his enormous gun over Lumu, resting it on the alien's shoulders. He could see no sign of the alien guard.

"He's standing still somewhere, that camouflage hiding him in the background," Noah panted.

"Not from me, Finn. He's straight ahead, about thirty yards. From the posture I'd say he has eyes on where he thinks you are. This one's good, Finn, but he's swaying with fatigue after that battering."

Chapter 60

"Mr President, are we okay to talk?" asked Vice President Hawlish. He knew he wasn't, and the conversation coming his way was going to be even more complicated than normal.

"Yes," came the tired reply. President Bentley looked drawn and haggard. The weight of the role had usually sat lightly on his shoulders compared to most men. But that time had passed. The pill boxes waited expectantly in front of him.

"Sir, we need the doctors to leave the room. This is way above their clearance." He nodded apologetically to the two White House medical staff as they left the room. The look he received as they passed was clear.

Keep it short.

"John, this has gone to hell. The Brits are confirming what our satellites and intelligence teams are telling us. There's a spaceship floating in that Scottish Forest. Just came up from the ground. It's completely absorbed all radar signals with no radio contact either. In fact, no communication whatsoever." Hawlish paused, wanting to see where the president would take this.

"Jack, I—" Bentley sucked in a slow breath, "My heart won't take the stress anymore. I will officially step down in the next few days. You don't need that hoo-hah going on while dealing with this. But I've put the call in to the Chiefs of Staff and advisors to the council. It's yours to solve, Jack. I am sorry."

164

Hawlish nodded. "Okay, I accept. Faced with where we are now, we need to stand strong. A united front against whatever storm is brewing."

"And Jack, watch General Marks like a hawk. That man has ambition but above all else a ruthless streak when it comes to money and resources for his space programme. If you're in the way when it comes to that alien tech, then he'll step on you on the way past."

Chapter 61

Spaceship, Garshellach Forest
16:45 GMT / 11:45 EST

"Open the door," shouted Zuri for the fifth time, bashing her hands where the door had been before. "I need to help my squad."

"I judge that you would be putting your life in danger. My directive is to maintain the life of the crew of this science exploration ship. You are now registered as crew, your life must be maintained," said the Hooded Voice, its tone robotic in manner as it repeated itself for the fourth time.

"If my squad dies, then my life is not worth living; they are my friends. They die, I die inside."

"I understand that is an idiom. Your language may be better than I thought. You mean you will suffer; your mental health relies on their survival."

"Yes, please open the door."

"Your physical state appears more than just the normal suffering due to physical exertion and injury. Though I don't know this up-to-date human body as well as I did your old ones, my examination suggests you are correct. I will open the door in five seconds."

A relieved Zuri crouched against the wall, the recessed edge of the doorway hopefully providing cover if the guard had remained where he was.

"Three, two, one."

The door quivered, releasing itself from the metal skin of the spaceship. It slid back, allowing Zuri a view of the earth mound she jumped over after releasing her last grenade. There, just the other side of the door, lay her assault rifle. She judged it to be just out of reach.

Zuri listened carefully at the edge of the door; the sound of the forest was bereft of gunfire. She did not know what to feel. The potential loss of Finn and the others sat heavy upon her. The words from *!Nias* grated against the rage his kind had caused. But the ring of desperation and truth prodded at her, stirring that sense of survival she wrapped her daily life around.

What would I have done in their shoes?

"To aid your likelihood of survival, there are three humans outside to the right of the door. One retains the body signature of *!Nias* and his clothing. It has its back to you and is standing still about twenty yards from the entrance, facing your people."

"Can you help?"

"No, I cannot take life when my crew's survival is not in danger. I have no useful external weapons, nor would I use them," stated the voice.

"If I go out there I'm in danger, correct?"

"Technically, yes."

"Good to know." Zuri dived through the door, trying hard to ignore the wound in her side. She reached for the assault rifle and rolled into the mound, bringing the muzzle round to bear where she judged the alien to be.

A flicker of movement gave it away; it heard her land and was spinning to face her. The camouflage rippled and she caught its silhouette against the vegetation behind. Zuri aimed a burst in that direction, then a second, before rolling back against the ship. The bullets fractured the back plate of its ceramic armour, the kinetic gel absorbing only some of the impact. The alien now faced her but a shot from Noah clipped its upper shoulder, enough to send it off balance. Zuri watched as a Finn exploded from behind the undergrowth, Lumu's Glock in hand. She squeezed to fire another burst as the alien fired energy bolts her way.

As Finn sprinted for the alien he saw the flame of the energy bolts arrow towards Zuri, her eyes wide as she saw death coming. The animal in him rose, and he landed both knees in the back of her killer. Placing the pistol against a hole in the plate he emptied the magazine through its spine. After the last bullet pummelled the body, Finn stood. Warily, his eyes sought Zuri, needing her, needing to see.

Before him the ship wall bulged and rippled. Its metallic skin briefly scarred, healed and smoothed over. As it reshaped itself back into the hull of the ship Zuri sat behind it, her assault rifle on her knees, eyes staring dully as if she'd faced her own death.

Finn ran over, gathering her in to his arms.

Alive.

"I can see this is going to be very stressful," filtered a voice through the ship door. "You humans haven't remotely calmed down in the last 33,000 years."

Chapter 62

Spaceship, Garshellach Forest
16:47 GMT / 11:47 EST

"We need to go inside, Finn," Smith talked calmly, slowly trying to wheedle his way past Finn's defensive walls as he held Zuri. *"Zuri's hurt and we are defenceless now."*

"Finn, I can hear Smith buzzing in your ear. I'm okay, just a wound in my side from before I went in the ship."

And a scar on my soul from our losses today.

"He's saying we should get in the spaceship, you're hurt, and we will struggle to defend ourselves. The weapons have rundown like a battery on constant use, or soon will do. They need a recharge and I suspect so does Smith, though he hasn't said that in case I'm tempted to accidentally forget."

"Humph."

Noah reached down with his hand and supported Zuri as she stood up. Without the adrenaline her side hurt like hell; she needed treatment though there was still no blood. She winced but carried on towards the door, Finn standing and following her. He stopped, turned around and went into the bushes as Smith twittered in his ear about the machine gun he'd dropped, shaking his head all the way. His foot hurt like hell, the burn mark across it from the energy bolt still smoked.

Zuri picked up her assault rifle; the squared metal piece had dulled and lost its lustre. She filed that information away for later as she let Noah help her through the door. When Zuri stepped through this time, she truly felt that she was entering a real spaceship. Before she had been forced in against her will. Now it was her choice.

Elfu huanzia moja. A thousand steps begin with just one.

They waited at the door until Finn returned. She didn't trust the world to deal her a fair hand any time soon. On his quick return with the machine gun and a cloth-wrapped parcel of alien weapons, he gave Zuri an appreciative shrug as he stepped through the door.

"These are not crew," announced the hooded voice. "They are not authorised to enter. And you need treatment right now. Crew are my priority. Please step through to the airlock door. These can stay here or leave as they please."

"Am I crew?" replied Zuri, knowing well enough how she was designated 'crew'.

"Yes, please attend to the airlock door. Palm print to confirm secondary security level entry."

"And if they follow me through?" Zuri was feeling belligerent, the pain not helping.

"They won't," stated the voice and as Zuri tried to reply the voice cut in, "I can bend walls, crew member, what else do you think I can do?" Though synthesised and mechanical, the voice added a tone of authority.

"How do we become crew?" asked Noah. "Is there a way we can be authorised?"

"Yes, you need the highest-ranking crew member to authorise your crew level access to the ship."

"Then who is in charge? Is there someone else on board we can talk to?"

"There is no one on board. Chief Xeno Scientist Crzz —… I can't repeat her name it uses a frequency too low for your hearing. She has not returned to set the next parameters for the ship. I am still designated for exploration despite the human access protocol, not yet as a SeedShip. Therefore, she is in charge but absent."

Noah was desperate to explore the information around the scientist but peering at Finn and Zuri confirmed this wasn't the time. He had come across many algorithms as awkward as this one before in his academic life. Though probably far more intelligent than anything he had encountered, it was not predictive; it appeared poor at actual leaps of problem solving. Everything had to be worked through logically, especially with variables like humans.

"So," Noah continued, "who is here as crew and in charge? You?"

"I cannot be in charge. I am not crew. I am an Artificial Intelligence limited by the Convention of the Haven Council. The registered crew member has not been named, but she stands next to you."

"So, Zuri can authorise us to become crew?" Noah pointed over to Zuri to make sure it understood who he meant.

Got there.

"Yes, yes she can," the voice paused but Noah knew something was coming as the penny dropped. "I apologise. I am not used to conversing with humans. My past crew used me for little else but flying and analysing data."

"I, Zuri Zuberi, wish to authorise these two humans as part of my crew. One Tobias Finn known only as Finn to everyone, and Stephen Noah." In response, four blue lights lit up next to them along the wall. "Place your palms on there," Zuri said with a nod of reassurance.

After the experience at the House, Finn and Noah expected the worst. What they got was the loss of blood and skin. Zuri tried to hide her smile despite the emotion of the day as she watched Finn gawk as his skin disappeared into the wall.

"Authorised," announced the hologram. "Opening the air lock door now."

Zuri stepped towards the door as it swung inwards, eager to see what lay inside.

Chapter 63

The Situation Room, Washington DC
16:52 GMT / 11:52 EST

"Anything to report, gentlemen?" asked Hawlish, uncomfortable in his new position and aware there was a big decision coming.

"The NATO air forces report numerous attempted inroads by Russian aircraft. They have turned back at least four intelligence gathering sorties. They are still circling in international airspace," replied General Brown. "Keeping detail from them is vital for our long-term strategy, I would say they are just at arm's length."

"They are steaming three of their naval ships towards the North Atlantic via the Norwegian Sea on a heading towards the Shetland Isles at the tip of Scotland. One is carrying their hypersonic missiles, the other covering frigates. We have submarines monitoring and the UK has a frigate on intercept course, which should reach the area within a few hours. The UK North Sea Fleet is in the area, about a day away if needed. Our ships are sailing in from the North Atlantic to provide support, time frame around two days before they are in effective range. The French are covering the English Channel. The Norwegians have their frigates on standby." Admiral Strang bowed his head as he finished his report.

"Sir, RAF Lossiemouth is running continuous sorties from their Quick Reaction interceptor squads. Supported by their helicopters patrolling for submarines," chipped in Brown. "These are split between keeping aircraft out of the area and as 'protests' about Russia's intent."

"We have reports from our army intelligence unit joint operation in

England. They say that the EMP multi-wave device has stopped transmitting. The British are contemplating sending in the Typhoons on reconnaissance and to support their AWACS. At the moment, other than basic visual satellite surveillance, we have nothing on that spaceship. There's no communication going in or out," added General Garcia, Chief of Staff for the Army.

"Do we have any detail on the aliens at all, or the SAS on intercept?"

"Satellite images are difficult, sir. Getting the X37B spaceplane over the UK was a delicate operation, politically and scientifically," General Marks said. "But the latest image from around five minutes ago shows bodies on the ground around the ship. A mix of Brits and the aliens. There are definitely aliens at large, and hopefully some of the SAS troop. We need more information, sir, and the satellite is not in geosynchronous orbit. Next image in ninety minutes; the Brits' satellite will have it in ten, if they share it."

"At the moment all we have is a spaceship hovering in the middle of a Scottish Forest. You don't know if anyone has gained entry, but the fact it has risen from under ground would say a big fat *yes*. We know the Brits haven't been hiding this thing, so we are left with a situation where an alien has possibly switched the damn thing on."

Hawlish watched the Chiefs of Staff nod in unison. They were not in control; the variables and implications were massively complex. Any action or interference on the USA's part would have political implications for years. But not to act could leave them in a dire mess; they could not risk other powers gaining the upper hand.

We need that technology, or worst case, we need no one else to get it.

"Recommendations?"

"We have discussed this at length," stated General Garcia, the current Chairman of the Chiefs of Staff. "At the moment we must assume the ship is hostile. All evidence points to an alien mission focussed on liberating that ship. Considering their military approach to this incursion, including the likely deaths of unarmed soldiers and the SAS, then we must assume it has significant military value to them. Though we feel it is unlikely that, on recovering the spaceship, they would choose to put it at risk; we are all in agreement that the spaceship will most definitely defend itself." Garcia took a breath whilst contemplating his next words. "It pains me to say it but we recommend standing off, sir. If we make the first strike, whatever we feel about the loss of our men, then we may face a battle we can't win."

Vice President Hawlish looked over to General Marks, who was nodding in agreement. He had expected Marks to be straining at the leash to get his hands on the tech inside that ship. Mind you, there were some juicy prizes already recovered according to the Brits, which he would relish.

"Are you saying that should it move off, we let it go? If it leaves without threatening any of the NATO countries or allies, we stand down?"

"Essentially yes; if it leaves, no one gets the tech. Including those we don't want to have it," replied Garcia. "But if they move to attack, then we need a full NATO reaction plan and I believe we have little time to make it."

"You have of course contemplated what happens if they return with more ships?" asked the Vice President.

"Yes," said General Marks of the US Space Force, "I have." Despite himself, and the trauma of the day's events, he felt a little thrill at the prospect of what this meant for his department.

Ah, there you are, General.

Chapter 64

When Zuri stepped inside the airlock door, she was struck by how simplistic the interior room appeared. Walls of similar blue-shaded metal curved over a central area from which open doorways lead out in all directions. The floor remained bronzed, though ribbons of a darker copper sheen rippled through them. On first glance the ribbons appeared to separate out, with a single strand flowing through each doorway. The room was set centrally, with oddly angled couches built from similar materials to those in the House. These were low-seated with high, curved backs, all looking inwards to a central dais. Zuri took that as the control system; from where she stood it appeared similar in structure to the panel Smith's hologram had arisen from in the House. She had expected to be wowed, surrounded by all the trappings of the movies she'd watched. But there were no flashing lights or panels of switches. Not even a command chair.

Bit underwhelming, really. Set up like a coffee morning. Is this the crew room?

Zuri stepped to the side to allow Noah and Finn through. Both scanned the room as she had, with Noah approaching the central dais with more interest than Zuri. Noah noted the raised metal panel on top of it with a sequenced pattern of squares and rectangular indents ready for the information plaques such as Smith's. Set at the side was a low shelf with carefully set-out slabs of the data holding metal, each labelled with a jumble of dashes and lines that, to his eye, had no pattern he could discern.

"Need a recharge, Finn, can you hand me over to Noah."

175

Smith sounded more distant to Finn, faded. Whatever the temptation level was to get Smith out of his ear, Finn had to admit they wouldn't have made it without him.

If I must.

"Here, Noah. Can you get Smith in place to charge up? I'll have a look for where the weapons can hook up to."

Finn handed over the helmet, bulky with the set of night vision goggles and the PRR radio. Noah removed Smith's plaque and slotted it in the correct-sized square. Finn slipped between the couches, heading for the racks and shelving he'd spotted against the left-hand wall near the airlock door.

"No! Out!" bellowed the Hooded Voice, its hologram appearing above the couches, hovering just below the central ceiling. "Get your claws out of my system." At that, Smith's plaque jumped from its slot to clattering on the dais edge before hitting the floor. Noah and Finn watched, stunned, as Smith's plaque came to a standstill flat upon the bronzed metal.

"Errr," started Noah as he reached down for the square metal containing Smith's persona. "Problem? This needs a recharge soon."

"That thing has no protocol. No, what's the word… manners. It tried to wheedle its way into my systems without even a 'hello'," said the robotic voice, managing a clearly indignant quality. "This is my data space; this is my ship to manage."

Zuri walked over; taking Smith from Noah's hand she slipped it on to the back of Finn's helmet. She handed it to Finn.

"You tell him to keep his hands off; recharge and communication only. And tell him I'm embarrassed by his actions. A corporal should know better."

"Nope, you tell him. He never listens to me." Finn took Zuri's helmet and slid his own on to Zuri's head. "And if you really want, you can keep him."

Zuri gave Finn her best withering look, one that Finn knew oh too well. He saluted and spun on the spot to finish the job he started, and to avoid the one he didn't want.

"I heard," spoke Smith through the earbuds. "Hands off, recharge only. I was only doing what I did at the House. I had no idea this AI is more aware." His voice was weak, but Zuri recognised the genuine hurt in there.

"Smith, the human recorded on this," Zuri tapped the metal plaque on the helmet as she looked towards the hologram, "is aware of what you expect. May he recharge?"

"If Zuri Zuberi has set the protocol, then yes, I agree. But I'll short his circuits if he tries it again."

"Oh, crap. I'll behave."

Zuri handed the helmet over to Noah and sat down with a gasp; her side was screaming for attention. She slipped off her combat armour to get a better look. As she undid the first buckle at her waist, she moved the burnt fatigues underneath with anxious hands. The hole beneath wasn't deep–the combat armour had taken the brunt from the alien's energy pistol–but it had penetrated under her ribs close to her liver. She saw Finn wince as he pretended to search for a weapons rack.

"Prepared treatment is in the med-lab, Zuri Zuberi. Please follow the glowing line," stated the holographic voice.

"Zuri. Please call me Zuri." She stumbled trying to get up from the couch; a strong hand caught her arm as Finn had returned to lift her up.

"As you wish, Zuri. Follow the pathway shown."

Leaning into Finn, Zuri moved away from the central console. The floor strips' purpose now obvious; one ribbon glowed with a warm light and led through a door on the opposite side of the airlock. Finn led Zuri in that direction, trusting what he had been told. Ten minutes ago he'd been in a firefight for his life and that of his squad. Now he was walking through a curved doorway in a spaceship seeking its med-lab. Every time he thought his day couldn't get any worse, or any stranger, something topped it off. At least now they weren't under fire.

And Zuri is safe.

The line slipped under a door with a curved top. The apparently random scratches and lines upon it resembled those on the data plaques. Finn nodded to Zuri and pushed at the low door handle that protruded from it, the design clearly set lower and for a larger hand than his.

"Please lay on the operating table," greeted the ship's AI as they walked through.

The lab appeared the very opposite of what they'd just been in. Panels and computer screens layered one wall; a mix of equipment lay strewn upon tables all with unknown purposes. But their appearance was not so far from the medical instruments they knew. What unsettled them both was the wall and ceiling covered in smooth-metalled robotic arms. Each had a different bladed attachment or mechanical hands with extended digits, the third finger much longer than the rest.

Finn swallowed his anxiety. The hologram had done nothing for him to be concerned about. In fact, it had saved Zuri's life, and so why would it harm her now? Zuri shifted herself towards the table, sitting down and swinging her legs up.

"I have analysed your cell structure and devised a medical—err, flesh graft. I think that is the nearest word. I have only just gained your DNA and therefore the synthesis is a little rushed. But I believe it will be effective. I will set a medical scan now to make sure my original data was correct. Sit back, Zuri."

Zuri followed the instructions. One of the robotic arms moved out much more smoothly than she expected. As she looked up and behind her, she could see the arm flowed through the wall rather than following any track or rail, seemingly part of it. Her mind flinched but settled as she remembered the protruding hull the AI had used to save her life. The mechanical limb ran above her, the instrument in its hand glowed with the blue light that seemed to be their common choice of colour. Zuri recognised there were subtleties in the shades they used, but her eyes struggled to differentiate these with any regularity. It just added to the strangeness. The scanner returned to its position.

"Confirmed. Initial analysis within expected boundaries. Zuri, we will now apply the plug. We must ensure you do not move; may I place restraints across your upper legs and waist?"

"Yes, go ahead. Do whatever you need to do." Her pain was rising; Zuri worried now that the energy bolt had seared something important. She needed the worry to go away, needed to know she would be alright. Finn tensed by her side, realising the adrenaline of the fight had camouflaged the seriousness of her wound.

"Permission received." The table grew restraints out from its side. These flipped over and merged into the flank of the operating table. Finn watched, stunned, as they pulled Zuri's lower body down and flat on to the table. One arm above Zuri dipped its limb in to the wall above her head, emerging with a mass of flesh, muscle and sinew between its fingers. As Finn watched, his body fought his mind for control. The urge to reach up and stop the arm from hurting Zuri causing tremors to run through his muscles.

"Tobias Finn, known as Finn to everyone. Your cortisol readings are rocketing. I have permission to do whatever is necessary from Zuri. I will not harm her. I protect my crew from harm as a primary objective."

Finn ran through his breathing exercises, counting slowly to ten as he did so. Zuri had given approval, so he had to respect that. A second limb descended and moved towards the wound; with delicate movements it cleaned and sprayed around it. The liquid hardened, leaving the wound slightly stretched open. The arm holding the graft gently moved above Zuri and eased it in to plug the wound. Zuri, her eyes closed, flinched slightly as it slid home. The second limb returned, sprayed the wound and placed what appeared to be a skin patch over the top. It adhered to the surrounding skin.

"Operation complete. You must rest, Zuri. I do not know how long the plug will take to be accepted by your body to begin the healing process. My understanding is based on Haven's medical records, and those are so out of date."

The medical scanner passed over her wound, returning to move back up and over her head. Zuri settled back and closed her eyes.

"Thank you," whispered Finn, "and it's just Finn. Rest Zuri."

"She is asleep, Finn. The scanner has soothed the electrical impulses in her brain to replicate a sleep pattern of eight hours." Finn looked up towards the hooded hologram, nodded, and left.

Chapter 65

Spaceship, Garshellach Forest
17:10 GMT / 12:10 EST

As Finn entered the central hub of the ship, he noted Smith's 3D image projecting from the central dais. The look on his face cheered Finn up just a little; clearly he was feeling sorry for himself. Chastised.

"It wasn't my fault. How was I supposed to know?"

Finn set a grim face and just shook his head. He said nothing, not wanting to give Smith any chance to make amends.

Let him stew a while.

Noah stood by a table at what Finn assumed was the wall nearest the front of the spaceship. He had laid the weapons out in to a set of grooves, the metal plaques containing their copies slotted beside them. They glowed another shade of blue, perhaps mixed with a tinge of green. It matched the colour of Smith's beneath him at the dais.

Noah's face was a picture, awe written across every pore. His body exuded excitement, babbling away to something set in the wall. As Finn got closer, the small image of the ship's AI came in to view, hovering over a plinth above the weapons.

"So, what you're saying is that this spaceship is from a planet 1800 light years away?" continued Noah. "That's an impossible distance to even imagine." Noah was trembling, practically hopping from foot to foot.

"Yes, if I had access to your current planetary data I could pinpoint exactly where it is. However, right now I am on external communication lockdown."

That garnered Finn's interest. They needed to get a message out to UK command about the situation.

"What do I call you?" he asked, looking directly at the small hologram over Noah's shoulder.

"Well, I don't have a name. The Haven never gave me one. I was just 'ship' to them, a concept rather than a name." The hologram shifted, changing its position to regard Finn from under its hood. "Most had communication implants.. They just 'thought' of me, and I responded. This spoken way of communicating was reserved for the non-scientists."

Finn nodded. "Okay, well I work best off names. I'm sure Zuri can come up with one. I need to get a message out to army command. I need them to know we have neutralised the aliens and taken control of this ship."

"Control? You must be mistaken. This ship belongs to the Haven. I have not been designated as a SeedShip yet. We await Chief Scientist Crr—" Finn felt his eardrums vibrate, almost a low, imperceptible hum just on the edge of what he could hear.

"Your Chief Scientist; I assume she lived in the House near to where you were left underground," stated Noah. "It was empty. There was no one there and I suspect there hadn't been for a very long time."

"They did not leave me underground. I was buried by a glacier and its moraine, the rock and rubble it left behind. I've been dormant, waiting for the signal to awaken."

Noah blinked and looked over to Finn as he spoke, "The last ice age would have covered Scotland about 33,000 years ago. You've been dormant all that time? Do you think your Haven Scientist will still be alive?"

The hologram froze, just the various shades of blue that made up the 3D image flickering as it stayed motionless. Noah raised his finger to Finn, asking for patience. He waited under sufferance; he was in a hurry but no quick answer came.

"Can you find out if they are alive?" asked Noah.

"I need to scan the planet," the AI uttered. "I need full information on where she is. Her Data Plaque will have her copied persona on it. If it is still active, I should be able to pick it up and make a rescue." The hologram winked out.

The airlock door slammed shut; Finn could sense the movement as a low rumble vibrated through his feet but there was no window or control panel evident, no screens to see what was happening.

"Smith! Any idea what's happening?" he shouted.

"I am only allowed brief surface data. We are moving upwards, probably around ten yards and climbing. The AI is sending radio and other wavelength signals across the area. It'll want height to allow for the Earth's curvature," said Smith, obviously enjoying being important again. "I think this may be a rocky ride."

Chapter 66

The Situation Room, Washington DC
17:15 GMT / 12:15 EST

"Mr Vice President, by all reports the spaceship is on the move vertically. The RAF Typhoons are shadowing. Their AWACS is reporting the instigation of low-wave radio signals from the ship. Thermal cameras show significant heat build-up at what are likely thruster points and the rear of the ship. It may be getting ready for full lift off," General Brown completed his report, weariness settling into his shoulders. "All NATO units are standing by as per the agreed plan. No signs of hostility, sir."

And may it stay that way.

"Any more information about the Russian Missile ship?" Hawlish stood at the head of the table holding his breath, the Russians were the random element in their plan.

"Their intelligence planes are still circling, sir; they are clearly feeding information to the Russian ships off Shetland. The British Frigate reports they are slowing down, possibly entering a holding pattern within the twenty-four nautical mile contiguous zone but not in UK's territorial waters. Playing a game, sir," stated Admiral Strang.

"Okay, do we have a projection on where this spaceship may go? What happens if it leaves and heads for orbit?"

"Well, it is most likely to travel from Scotland on a curving eastward projection. This takes advantage of the Earth's rotation, minimising issues around fuel. This would likely take it over Scandinavia and on towards," said General Marks, looking at the room as the pieces slotted together in his head, "Russia."

"Is anyone else thinking what I'm thinking? The single greatest opportunity in human history is about to fly right out of our hands and land in Russian laps. If you think they'll have any qualms about knocking that ship out of the sky to land on their territory, then you are in the wrong job." The Vice President sat down heavily, exhausted.

The room was silent, their plans already set in motion. They had agreed to wait, to see if they were under threat. Their hands tied by politics as much as morality.

Chapter 67

The Haven spaceship continued to rise further, reaching one hundred yards above the forest floor. The AI pinged its call of hope on its standard low radio frequency, but now adjusted and sent signals far and wide across all wave bands on the spectrum. Its radar and light sensors threw back more than enough information about the approaching aircraft, recognising the weapons of war housed within.

"We have approaching atmospheric craft, all armed. Crew to take safety stations," called the AI; as it spoke, the surrounding floor swirled. The couches merged into the deck, melting away as two command chairs formed in their place, growing from the floor. Whatever else was happening, Noah and Finn had the sense to know the purpose of the chairs.

"What about Zuri?" shouted Finn; the room was almost silent, he needed to be heard.

"Zuri is safe, strapped in. Prime objective is crew safety," came the reply.

Finn and Noah both jumped in their chairs, the padding adjusting around them as they sat back. They felt immobilised but protected by the cushioning. Straps flew across shoulders, ends integrating back into the seat chassis.

"Evasive actions prepped. Atmospheric manoeuvres will cause unstable internal movements. Crew be aware."

"How do you know they are hostile?" asked Noah. "They could be ours. There could be no threat to the crew."

"I have no parameters for 'ours'. Idiom analysis incomplete. You say these aircraft could belong to you personally, yet they fly towards us with weapons? No time, flight path established."

The spaceship moved, then accelerated fast. Finn felt the drive right through his teeth and bones, his skin feeling stretched. Noah was grinning, the acceleration stretching the smile from ear to ear until the tunnel vision started. Finn was sure he heard a short but strangled whoop of joy.

"Reducing acceleration effects; sorry, human crew, but you will experience sustained acceleration at a rate of four times your planet's gravity, less than half of our current rate."

Smith had a look of complete consternation on his face. Finn sensed he had something to say but was keeping it to himself. He was receiving some information; he'd stated that earlier. But at this level of acceleration there was no way Finn could ask–even breathing was difficult.

"Missiles detected, launch imminent. Launched, calculating maximum acceleration and speed. Ultra-high-speed capabilities detected. Intercept established. These 'yours' too, Noah?" Noah had already blacked out, unable to respond. Finn clamped his mouth together, trying to hold on to consciousness, not letting the blackness engulf him.

"Unable to increase acceleration in case of harm to crew. Missiles on intercept. Will make contact in thirty seconds. Establishing nano-shields."

Finn braced, counting down the seconds. As he hit twenty-four the ship lurched, dropping sharply and banking right. At thirty the ship stuttered in the air, shifted again, then continued along its path.

"Missile contact and neutralised. Loss of ship's nano mass five per cent, re-establishing hull integrity. Finn, you remain conscious. My sensors show further missile launches ahead, contact likely over the land mass named Russia on the new information stream. Crew safety is paramount. Please advise."

"Advise?" Finn mouthed the word as best he could.

"Permission to act as I see fit. This will engage the return protocol."

"Granted," Finn mouthed as he finally lost consciousness.

Chapter 68

The Situation Room, Washington DC
17:20 GMT / 12:20 EST

The room was completely silent, stunned. Exhaustion and anxiety poured from the men sat around the table. The Vice President's phone rang; he picked it up and listened intently.

"Ah, gentlemen. I apparently have the Russian Presidential advisors on the phone wanting to establish a line to discuss the situation. If you would please gather as much intelligence as you can, and we'll meet, say, around 5pm? Maybe grab some sleep, too."

The Vice President spun his chair wearily and placed the phone briefly to his ear before changing his mind and setting it down on silent.

"And Generals, get me that damn EMP weapon. I want it; we need it if there's anything good to come out of this. Am I clear? That weapon could be the end of the established military world as we know it. Promise the UK military whatever they want but we need their full cooperation on this. And I want it nailed down as tight as a drum. No leaks, no mess-ups. China and Russia will know damn well what happened and they'll be quaking in their boots, but they'll stop at nothing to get hold of it."

This is a moment in time humanity will never forget.

Hostile Contact.

Chapter 69

Spaceship, nr Jupiter
Two days after leaving Earth

Zuri twitched; a light blow of air caressed her nose then faded away. She rubbed at the spot and turned over. Another light tingle rippled across her shoulder, then her neck. Zuri swatted at it as her brain tried to drag her out from a deep sleep. She rolled herself back over and slowly opened her eyes. A robotic hand resolved itself amongst the initial blur in her vision. One long finger pointing towards her, its tip open to reveal a tube blowing gentle air.

"What the…" Zuri sat up, slowly realising the restraints had gone.

My wound.

As she scrambled to lift her t-shirt, she realised she was no longer in combat fatigues. There was no scar; prodding, she could feel no pain. Zuri scanned the room, then slipped off the table. She was barefoot; the bronzed floor felt warm to the touch. It was soft, not hard like she expected at all. In fact, it was quite pleasant to walk on.

Zuri pushed open the door and padded down the short corridor to the central hub. She was eager to see Noah and Finn and find out what had happened over the last few hours while she slept. As she stepped through the entrance, the room appeared different to how she remembered.

Have I gone a little crazy?

In the middle of the room lay Noah and Finn, both in eased-back, command-type chairs. Their eyes were closed; they were clearly asleep. They wore a similar black t-shirt and joggers as she did. As she studied them,

Zuri could see that Noah's burn mark upon his cheek had healed and his arm was clear of the shrapnel wound. All the bruises and minor scratches they had suffered had healed. She reached upwards towards her own cuts around neck and arm from her first encounter with the aliens. All gone.

"Zuri," said the AI voice, "they remain asleep. I deemed it necessary to remove any potential harm as we left Earth's orbit at a high acceleration rate. Sleep made this easier for all of you."

The AI appeared in front of Zuri, establishing the same height as her in its blue light form. It wore a layered robe, the cowl still shrouding the head. In Zuri's sleep-addled mind, the words only just filtered through.

"Left Earth's orbit? What do you mean left orbit?"

"We were under attack by numerous missiles. My ship mass would likely not sustain the number of strikes and be one hundred percent sure of crew safety. Finn, as the only conscious crew member, gave permission for me to enact the safety protocols."

"And these involve leaving Earth's orbit?" Zuri passed on her incredulous look towards the AI.

"Well, yes and no. They give me permission to act as I see best in operation of the ship. The Haven are absolute in their commitment to individual survival. Establishing an AI to oversee their safety can be an effective practice in certain circumstances. But the Convention dictates a ship must return to the home world when this happens to ensure it is not the AI that is endangering life, and for any required crew rebirth. I am locked out of the navigation controls. We are heading back to Havenhome."

"I... I simply don't know what to say to that. We're heading to another planet? How long... where..."

"It may be best if I answer these questions when they are awake. I woke you first as I need you."

"It sure does," stated Smith, appearing at the dais. "You should see what's coming." As he did so the AI turned to face his hologram, clicked her fingers and the data plaque jumped from its slot.

"I need to integrate with my new crew. There are no Haven aboard, and you are a visual and auditory species with no implants." The AI removed the cowl, revealing a human female face, one Zuri recognised. "I took this image from your persona recording. I believe it is an old friend, Yasuko?"

Zuri nodded. "Yes, Yasuko. She told me it meant peaceful. One of my friends from the county gymnastic sessions. If you are asking my permission, I have no issues. She is a beautiful person, though much feistier than her name suggests."

"Perfect."

Chapter 70

Spaceship, approaching Saturn
Four days after leaving Earth

Zuri lay spread across her couch, the plush upholstery soft against her cheek. It was an exact copy of her favourite settee from home where she'd spent many a Saturday morning watching tv as a child. On the view screen along the wall Saturn slowly span, a truly awesome sight with the near-perfect icy rings wrapping round the gaseous planet. Zuri had lain there for a time every day since awakening, letting the view reframe her new reality.

I am in space, I did encounter aliens, I have survived.

The shock and grief overwhelmed her on that first day. After she had spoken to Yasuko, everything seemed to hit her in a storm of anguish and loss. The trainees, the soldiers she had fought alongside, Lieutenant Bhakshi, who despite the stick up his arse had been there for Finn and saved him from the self-dug pit he was crawling in to. All gone.

Zuri found she felt no guilt, had let no one down. She had fought as hard as anyone and been there for her squad. She could have done no more. But there was a hole in her heart where those people should have been. Zuri examined the tattoo along her hand, the semi-colon she'd had done as soon as she was old enough.

And I endure.

Memories would fade, and it was this that nagged at her now. In her dreams she saw *!Nias*, his large eyes beseeching her help. Zuri owed him nothing, he had attacked her world. The blood of her people was on his hands.

But do we let an entire people fade away, his !ke? Is that who I am now?

"Can we talk?" asked Smith, his image hovering above the central console.

Zuri and Smith had said little to each other over the past few days. She had accepted that he was Smith, or as much as she could allow herself to in this new reality. His memories and mannerisms were the same. But his personality seemed at odds with itself, as if he was wrestling with his emotions all the time, unsure of what tact to take.

"Go ahead, I'm sorry I have been a little distant."

"Grief. I feel that, too." Smith's hologram sat down in the projected image; he gave a virtual sigh. "I don't know what I am, Zuri. I contain everything I was and am, but it's disconnected. I am on the outside of myself looking in. When we were in combat, my focus was on keeping you all alive, doing what was right. But I am not a corporal any more, just the ghost of one. And it hurts."

"Maybe you need to talk to Yasuko. Her understanding of you as a…"

"Say it, I can't hide from it. As a copy, a recording. Data," Smith spat out each painful word.

"Yes. But from the hints she has given there may be more to it. You need to rebuild bridges with her. Try treating her like a person, not a computer."

Smith nodded, his head hung low in his hands. Zuri could feel the sadness, despite him only being the light and shade of a hologram.

He needs something to focus on other than himself.

"If you don't, you will only fester on it. What are we doing about Noah and Finn? Are we waking them up soon?"

"You mean before the transition to Havenhome?" Smith replied, looking directly at Zuri now.

"Yes, before that. I have spent the last few days staring at Saturn trying to understand what's happening. If we wake them afterwards, they won't have anything familiar to anchor themselves to. I should have woken them earlier."

If I hadn't been selfish and needed the time and space to start healing.

"I think, knowing Finn as I do, beforehand would be better. Give him time to complain about his lot before getting on with it." Smith threw a small grin to Zuri. He couldn't resist a dig. "And Noah would probably just enjoy the ride."

Zuri nodded. "No time like the present. Yasuko?"

"Here," the AI said, appearing as she commonly did now, as a full-size human. "Can I help?"

"Yes, I think it's time we woke the others. Smith and I agree they need to be awake for the transition. Are you okay with that?"

* * *

Finn leaned back in his chair. The last few days had come as an initial shock to him; he was millions of miles from home. But then again, he was alive. He survived an alien assault–two assaults, even–and come away with his life. The losses on the way he needed to grieve. But he had Zuri, and there were so many moments that he'd thought she was lost amongst the chaos of the day. Noah, too. It was time to find out what came next after Zuri had given them some space to mull over what they'd been through; it sounded ominous.

Zuri looked across to Finn and Noah. Their story together was not over, and after a few days rest they needed to know what was coming. After all, in a way, Finn had set it in motion. The viewing screens established on the reformed walls, it had almost become normal now to see them emerge.

"Permission to engage the return protocol, she asked him," said Zuri, facing Noah and Finn, who sat on their chairs in front of the viewscreen. "Granted, he replied. Did he stop to ask what it was? Oh no. No questions passed his lips."

Saturn's perfect rings lay defined in front of them, the icy chunks mottled with rocks and dust. The planet swirled with patterned gases as it rotated within. Zuri moved into their view, pointing to the screen.

"This is Titan. In about two hours we will establish an orbit around it. Then, according to my new friend Yasuko," the AI, newly formed as Zuri's old friend from her gymnastic days, stepped in to view as instructed, "we are going on a joy ride 1800 light years in this direction." The screen pulled back from Saturn, accelerating past Uranus and Neptune and on through the Oort Cloud. It swirled through numerous star systems before coming to rest, looking down upon a single planet composed of a beautiful mix of green, blues and browns, with strips of cloud whirling above. The shock and joy on Noah's face was a picture to behold, in contrast to the sheer misery on Finn's.

"Tighten your seatbelts and kiss your arse goodbye. We're going on the lightspeed express!" shouted Yasuko. "Did I say that right, Zuri?"

"Near enough," nodded Zuri, "near enough."

The End of Hostile Contact: Book One of the Weapons of Choice Series

About the Author

Thank you for choosing to spend your precious time getting to the end of my book. If you got this far, then my hope is that you enjoyed the ride just as much as I enjoyed writing it.

Reviews are the lifeblood for any author, and it would be greatly appreciated if you would take the time to write a few words and help spread the message about this first book in the Weapons of Choice series. Your words and thoughts are precious. Not only do they keep me going during the dark, lonely nights, but your review may fuel a passion for action packed sci-fi in lost souls still searching for their next read. Think of a review as starlight in the void of space, drawing in those lost in the mire of the real world. Be that light.

https://www.amazon.com/dp/B0BXQ4L99W (USA)
https://www.amazon.co.uk/dp/B0BXQ4L99W (UK)

You can also find out a little bit more about the future of the series at www.nicksnape.com and join the mailing list that will keep you up to date about forthcoming books and the 'soon to be completed' free subscriber Novella. I have led a very boring life, living my adventures through books and gaming, but for those interested, I have detailed a little about myself there too.

And Finally

Though I would not profess to be an expert on all things mental health, my many years working with traumatised and neurodiverse children have given me a wide understanding of what children, young adults and adults go through in their daily lives.

In this work of fiction, I have highlighted some causes and symptoms of PTSD and by no means would I wish to belittle the hugely debilitating effects it has on many of our veterans and the traumas they face. For anyone wishing to learn more about this condition, there are many sources of information and charities out there on the web.

Also by Nick Snape

Return Protocol: Weapons of Choice Book 2 will be out in early April.

Join soldiers Finn, Zuri and Corporal Smith (deceased) as they battle a hostile First Contact that takes them to the very edge of sanity and the universe beyond in this character driven, heart-pounding military sci-fi adventure.Aliens, they are more like us than you think.

Printed in Great Britain
by Amazon

19659339R00120